NOW MORE WAYS TO ENJOY HISTORICAL FICTION!

HISTORICAL TIMES MAGAZINE
www.historicaltimes.org

THE HISTORICAL FICTION COMPANY
www.thehistoricalfictioncompany.com

HISTORY BARDS PODCAST
www.historybards.com

HIGH QUALITY EDITORIAL REVIEWS
www.thehistoricalfictioncompany.com/book-reviews

AWARD-WINNING CONTEST EXCLUSIVELY FOR HISTORICAL FICTION
www.thehistoricalfictioncompany.com/award-submission

Plus more - blog tours with

The Coffee Pot Book Club, an online bookshop,

author profiles, and an on-staff graphic design company

for your book cover, banner ads, and book trailer needs.

HISTORICAL TIMES

MAGAZINE

EDITOR-IN-CHIEF
DEE MARLEY

FOUNDER
SAM TAW

CONTRIBUTORS
ROS BARBER
ALISON WEIR
TONY RICHES
BONNIE G. SMITH
D. G. MACDOUGALL
D. K. MARLEY
NAOMI MILLER
ELIZABETH KEYSIAN
ELIZABETH WINKLER

SPONSORS
HELENA P. SCHRADER
SUSANNE DUNLAP
TOM DURWOOD
TESS THOMPSON
BOOKOUTURE

HFC REVIEWERS
DEE M.
BEVERLEE S.
BEVERLY Y.
JESSICA V.
DAVID S.
JULIAN D.
MICHAEL Z.
NICOLE P.
CHELSEA B.
JANE P.
CAMELIA K.

INTRODUCTION

The founder, Sam Taw, had a vision of an exclusive magazine devoted to historical fiction. After eighteen issues, her vision came to fruition and we at HFC are proud to continue her dream on into the future. Incorporating her talented designs into HFC's own brand, we hope you enjoy turning the pages as the magazine makes this historic transition.

OUR STATEMENT

We at HFC are dedicated to providing exclusive content and quality editorial reviews, articles, and resources for all historical fiction authors, aspiring writers, and readers across the globe.

CONTACT US

Address
—

MACON, GEORGIA 31211
U.S.A.

E : thehistoricalfictioncompany@gmail.com
W : thehistoricalfictioncompany.com
W : historicaltimes.org

COVER DESIGN BY WHITE RABBIT ARTS
Images by Shutterstock

Hi everyone! This issue is reaches straight to my heart as I've always been a lover of all things Tudor or Elizabethan-related. Long ago, at least twenty-five years ago, I stumbled upon the possibility that Shakespeare was not Shakespeare, and I was presented with the other candidates of authorship. Well, needless to say, my mind was blown as I had always been an avid Shakespearean. This set my feet on the path of researching and combined with my love of writing, my first historical novel started taking shape. Of course, years in the making as the research, the writing, the editing... and so on... enveloped me. I was inspired by reading Ros Barber's novel-in-blank-verse "The Marlowe Papers" and discovered a kindred spirit, one who also believed in the Marlowe-theory; and slowly my own words took shape. I am humbled to have Dr. Barber featured in this issue after all of these years, and I hope you enjoy the jammed-packed issue full of Tudor and Elizabethan delights.

D. K. Marley
CEO of The Historical Fiction Company & Historical Times
Magazine - Host / History Bards Podcast

Don't forget that our authors are based all across the globe, so there will be a mixture of US, UK, Australian, French, and Canadian spelling and grammar. You can expand pages to see the text using the zoom function and move them around the screen. You can also alter how many notifications you receive from us by accessing your account settings. You'll find the settings by clicking on the dropdown arrow next to your name after you have logged into the website.

Permissions and Rights
All HT logos, artwork and original material remain the property of Historical Times. No content may be copied, stored, transferred or shared without prior permission.
Contributors retain all rights over their own articles and features, with permissions granted to the Historical Times Magazine and community website for their limited use. See our policies page for more information. Historical Times takes no responsibility for the content of external websites linked to this or any other issue.

Why not become a part of the discussion?
Our WEBSITE is packed with articles,
discussions, interviews, and much more.

As a subscriber, you have access to all the current
and past issues of the magazine, and will hear about
online events, special deals and offers first.

FOLLOW US ON SOCIAL MEDIA   

A LOOK INSIDE

A rare portrait of Elizabeth prior to her accession, attributed to William Scrots. It was painted for her father in c. 1546. Image from Wikipedia

SAVING CHRISTOPHER MARLOWE

ROS BARBER

What do you know about Christopher Marlowe? Some will say he was a playwright in Shakespeare's time. Some will say he was gay, recalling the famous line about 'tobacco and boys'. The more knowledgeable will mention that he wrote the play Doctor Faustus or that he's the author of the poem that begins 'Come live with me and by my love.' They might tell you he was the bad boy of Elizabethan theatre, and that he died in a tavern brawl. But very little of this is true.

History is a collection of stories we tell about the past, and like all stories told repeatedly, they can get bent out of shape. Marlowe's public story began to get told, and distorted, in the last year of his life. In the immediate aftermath of his apparent death at Deptford in May 1593, his reputation took a beating from which it never recovered. I'm not here to whitewash a complex character, but I'd like to set the record a little straighter than it has been for the last 430 years.

Let's begin with that 'tavern brawl'. The phrase is so famous that it's indelibly linked with Marlowe's name. 'Drunken brawl' was an assumption made by the author of his entry in the Dictionary of National Biography thirty years before Marlowe's inquest document was unearthed in 1925 and the real story began to unfold. Mrs Bull's house, where Marlowe is said to have died, wasn't a tavern. Eleanor Bull was the great-niece of Blanche Parry, Queen Elizabeth I's most trusted gentlewoman-in-waiting. Mrs Bull was referred to as a 'cousin' by Lord High Treasurer Burghley, the Queen's chief advisor. According to Marlowe's biographer David Riggs, her house was most likely a government safe house; a stopping off-point for intelligence agents travelling to and from the continent.

Three of the men present at Mrs Bull's House that day were agents. Robert Poley was the senior operative. He and another of the three, Nicholas Skeres, had helped unmasked the Catholic conspirators of the Babington Plot. Marlowe was the third agent present.

That the playwright worked for the secret service is now well-established. A letter sent from five of the Queen's Privy Councillors to Cambridge University when he was 23, 'certifies' that Marlowe had "done her Majesty good service, & deserved to be rewarded for his faithful dealing," adding "it was not her Majesty's pleasure that anyone employed as he had been in matters touching the benefit of his Country should be defamed by those that are ignorant in the affairs he went about." The lack of punishment after Marlowe was arrested for counterfeiting in what is now the Netherlands, argues for his continued government service five years later. Betrayal during that mission by a double agent led Marlowe inexorably to Deptford the following year.

Whatever happened at Mrs Bull's house, it wasn't a brawl. That it was an accidental killing stemming from an argument over the bill (they'd eaten two meals during the nine-or-so hours

ME DESTRVIT

THE
Tragedie of Dido
Queene of Carthage:
Played by the Children of her
Maiesties Chappell.
Written by Christopher Marlowe, and
Thomas Nash. Gent.

Actors
Iupiter,   Ascanius.
Ganimed,   Dido.
Venus,   Anna.
Cupid,   Achates.
Iuno,   Ilioneus.
Mercurie or   Iarbas.
Hermes,   Cloanthes.
Æneas,   Sergestus.

Tamburlaine
the Great.
Who, from a Scythian Shephearde,
by his rare and woonderfull Conquests,
became a most puissant and migh-
tye Monarque.
And (for his tyranny, and terrour in
Warre) was tearmed,
The Scourge of God.

Deuided into two Tragicall Dis-
courses, as they were sundrie times
shewed vpon Stages in the Citie
of London.

By the right honorable the Lord
Admyrall, his seruantes.

Now first, and newlie published.

LONDON.
Printed by Richard Ihones: at the signe
of the Rose and Crowne neere Hol-
borne Bridge. 1590.

The troublesome
raigne and lamentable death of
Edward the second, King of
England: with the tragicall
fall of proud Mortimer:
As it was sundrie times publiquely acted
in the honourable citie of London, by the
right honourable the Earle of Pem-
brooke his seruants.
Written by Chri. Marlow Gent.

TRAGE
OF
THE RICH
OF MALT
AS IT WAS P
BEFORE THE KING AND
QVEEN, IN HIS MAJESTIES
Theatre at White-Hall, by her Majesties
Servants at the Cock-pit.

Written by CHRISTOPHER MARLO.

LONDON;
Printed by I. B. for Nicholas Vavasour, and are to be sold
at his Shop in the Inner-Temple, neere the
Church. 1633.

The Tragicall Historie o
the Life and Death of
Doctor Faustus.
With new Additions.
Written by CH. MAR.

Printed at Londo
the

THE
MASSACRE
AT PARIS:
With the Death of the Duke
of Guise.
As it was plaide by the right honourable the
Lord high Admirall his Seruants.
Written by Christopher Marlow.

AT LONDON
Printed by E. A. for Edward White, dwelling neere
the little North doore of S. Paules
Church at the signe of
the Gun

they spent together) is the least likely scenario. They met at ten, had dinner, walked in the garden, came in at six and had supper. The Queen's coroner, who conducted the inquest, reported that Marlowe, lying on a bed directly behind the bench on which the other three were sitting with their backs to him, had grabbed Ingram Frizer's dagger and hit him on the top of the head with the hilt of it, and that Frizer, trapped between the other two, had somehow twisted around and forced that same knife through Marlowe's eye. The actions described defy attempts to re-enact them, and the facts surrounding that all-day meeting leave a number of awkward holes.

The three men on whose testimony the inquest rests were all professional liars. The one not known to be in the secret service (Frizer) had a side-hustle with Skeres, conning foolish gentlemen out of their riches. Frizer, was a lifelong servant of Marlowe's patron Thomas Walsingham, who himself had worked for the intelligence network set up by his cousin Sir Fran-cis Walsingham. Frizer was pardoned with exceptional haste by the Queen, and was subsequently rewarded by Walsingham with land and leases in reversion.

There is another question-mark around Robert Poley's movements. Poley was an expert in entering other countries by stealth. An official warrant says he was carrying urgent letters for the Queen from the Hague and though she was only 12 miles when he was in Deptford on the inquest day, he took another week to deliver them. The warrant for Poley's payment for the month to June 8th (covering the death on the 30th May and the inquest on the 1st June, as well as his absence) states, in an phrase unique among the other warrants listed, that he was "in her

The corner of Old Court of Corpus Christi College, Cambridge, where Marlowe stayed while a Cambridge student and, possibly, during the time he was recruited as a spy Image by Wikipedia

Majesty's service all the aforesaid time."

Given that Marlowe had recently been arrested on serious charges that could lead to his torture or even execution, and given the combination of people present at Deptford, it's unlikely the occasion was a social gathering. And why was the listing of accusations against him retitled by the Lord Keeper into strangely equivocal language before being sent to Her Highness? Something else was afoot. The event that ended up with a bloody-faced corpse may have been an accident, or a cover-up for assassination, or a cover-up for escape, but it certainly wasn't a brawl.

Marlowe's reputation for being a 'brawler' doesn't rest on Deptford alone. But there is no evidence he was even as violent as his peers. The three incidents used to argue that he was have been mischaracterised after being read through the lens of a violent death.

The fight in 'Hog Lane' for example, was from its location mostly like a duel, a required defence of a gentleman's honour. (Marlowe had gained the status of gentleman when he received his MA.) The man he fought, William Bradley, had a history of violence, as well as an ongoing legal dispute with two of Marlowe's friends. One of them, Thomas Watson, arrived and took over the 'bout' (as it was described). It was Watson rather than Marlowe who killed Bradley, and both men's pleas of self-defence were accepted. Marlowe never killed or wounded anyone. Ben Jonson, by contrast, was found guilty of manslaughter, and had 'T' for Tyburn branded on his thumb. Johnson only escaped the noose because he could recite his 'neck verse' (Psalm 51); educated men were too valuable in Elizabethan society to be disposed of. Johnson was also said to have put a boy's eye out. Ben Jonson killed and maimed, but we do not consider him violent because he died fat and happy in his bed.

Similarly, Marlowe being bound over to keep the peace in May 1592 after a disturbance in Holywell Street doesn't necessarily imply violence; it may have been a loud argument. The common legal phrase associated with such an order, ob metum mortis, "for fear of death," is absent. This expression was, however, used when William Shakespeare was subjected to the same order in 1596. Biographers do not use it to portray Shakespeare as violent. There is also no evidence of physical violence when tailor William Corkine tried to sue Marlowe for damage to clothing in Canterbury. A close examination of court records shows that Corkine was a serial litigant who provoked arguments with people and then attempted to sue them for profit.

Can we at least agree Marlowe was gay? No, to be honest, we can't. We haven't got any hard evidence of his sexuality. Unlike Francis Bacon's brother Anthony, he was never in danger of being prosecuted for sodomy (which was a capital crime). Nor did he write about being anyone's 'bedfellow', as Gabriel Harvey did of the poet Edmund Spencer. We can hardly trust double-agent Richard Baines, who included "all they that love not tobacco and boys were fools" in his list of Marlowe's alleged outrages and blasphemies. Not only is this the unreliable testimony of Marlowe's mortal enemy, it may have been a mishearing. Marlowe's actual words may have been the more usual pairing "tobacco and booze." "Booze" was a new word then (with an early use by Marlowe's friend Thomas Nashe), so easy for the older man Baines to misinterpret. Certainly, in Marlowe's Edward II we have the sympathetic portrayal of gay king, but this is, like Shakespeare's portrayal of Richard II, simply a nuanced characterisation based on historical sources. Writers are not interchangeable with their characters. The truth is, we simply don't know Marlowe's sexuality.

It's a truism that history is written by the victors. In Marlowe's case, those victors were religious fanatics such as Thomas Beard, who slandered him in a best-selling book, stating he was killed 'in the theatre of God's judgements'. The good reputation Marlowe had among friends, and at the highest level of Government circles, where he'd been described as "orderly", "discrete" and "faithful", was destroyed at Deptford, and perhaps through no fault of his own. Marlowe was an intellectual questioner and free-thinker – dangerous in the totalitarian regime of Elizabeth's late reign. But we have no good evidence that he was a violent hothead. It is more than 400 years too late for Marlowe himself to be saved, but it's perhaps not too late to save his reputation.

DEATH'S A GREAT DISGUISER

Church-dead. And not a headstone in my name.
No brassy plaque, no monument, no tomb,
no whittled initials on a makeshift cross,
no pile of stones upon a mountain top.
The plague's the excuse; the age's curse
that swells to life as spring gives way to summer,
to sun, unconscious kisser of a warmth
that wakens canker as it wakens bloom.

Now fear infects the wind, and every breath
that neighbour breaths on neighbour in the street
brings death so close you smell it on the stairs.
Rats multiply, as God would have them do.
And fear infects like mould; like fungus, spreads -
folk catch it from the chopped-off ears and thumbs,
the burning heretics and eyeless heads
that slow-revolve the poles on London Bridge.

The child of casual violence grows inured,
an audience too used to real blood;
they've watched a preacher butcher, still awake,
and handed his beating heart like it was love.
And now the sanctioned butchery of State
breed sadists who delight to man the rack
reduce men from divine belief and brain
to begging, and the rubble of their spines.

From all this, I am dead. Reduced to ink
that magicks up my spirit from the page:
a voice who knows what mortals cannot think of;
a ghost, whose words ring deeper from the grave.....
READ MORE BY CLICKING THE BUY LINK

ROS BARBER

Ros Barber is an English novelist and poet. She is also a university lecturer in English, who supports the view that Christopher Marlowe wrote Shakespeare. As of 2021, Barber lectures in the Department of English and Comparative Literature at Goldsmiths, University of London. She has a BSc in Biology, an MA in creative writing, the arts and education, and a PhD in English literature, all from the University of Sussex. She also has an Open University BA in English literature and philosophy. She won the Hoffman Prize in 2011, 2014 and 2018. Barber's first novel, The Marlowe Papers (2012), is written in blank verse. She subscribes to the Marlovian theory of Shakespeare authorship. In the book, Marlowe's death is a ruse and he writes plays in Shakespeare's name. The book won the Desmond Elliott Prize and the Authors' Club First Novel Award. Her second novel, Devotion (2015), was shortlisted for the Encore Award. Barber made an appearance at the Brighton Fringe in 2012. She and Nicola Haydn wrote a one-man stage adaptation of The Marlowe Papers performed in 2016.

www.rosbarber.com

BUY THE BOOK
at AMAZON

Winner of the
2013 Desmond Elliott Prize
Longlisted for the
2013 Women's Prize for Fiction

You're the author of the greatest plays of all time.
But nobody knows.
And if it gets out, you're dead.

On May 30, 1593, a celebrated young playwright was killed in a tavern brawl in London. That, at least, was the official version. Now Christopher Marlowe reveals the truth: that his "death" was an elaborate ruse to avoid a conviction of heresy; that he was spirited across the English Channel to live on in lonely exile; that he continued to write plays and poetry, hiding behind the name of a colorless man from Stratford□ one William Shakespeare.

With the grip of a thriller and the emotional force of a sonnet, this remarkable novel in verse gives voice to a man who was brilliant, passionate, and mercurial. A cobbler's son who counted nobles among his friends, a spy in the Queen's service, a fickle lover and a declared religious skeptic, Christopher Marlowe always courted trouble. In this memoir, love letter, confession, and settling of accounts, Ros Barber brings Christopher Marlowe and his era to vivid life in *The Marlowe Papers*.

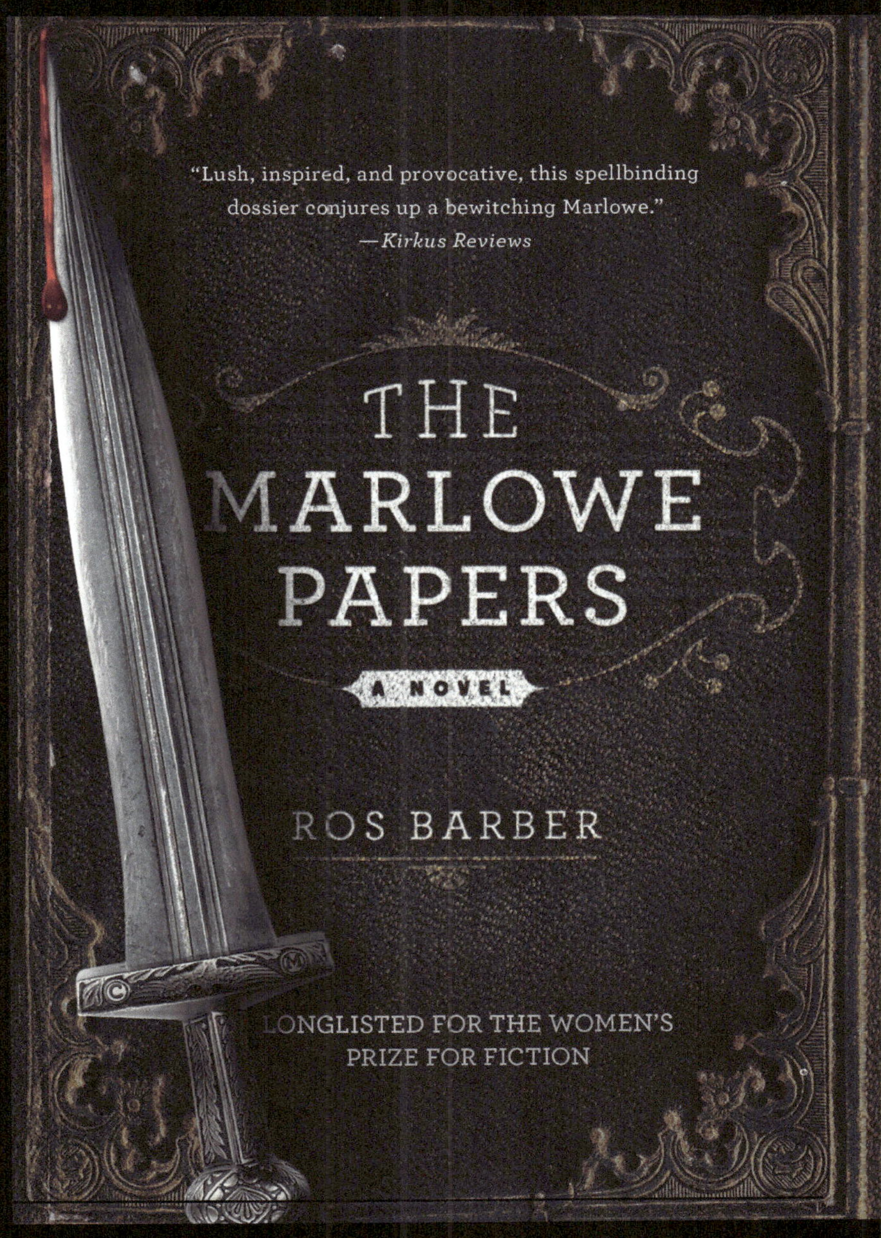

I am a Londoner, born and bred at Westminster, although I have also lived in Norfolk, Sussex, and Scotland, and now reside in Surrey. I have been married to Rankin Weir since 1972, and have two children, John (born 1982) and Kate (born 1984). I was educated at the City of London School for Girls, obtaining A-levels in English Literature, Art, and History (English and European medieval history, with twelfth-century monasticism in the West as my specialist subject), then at the North Western Polytechnic of London, where I trained as a teacher with History as my main subject, studying world history, English medieval history, and the Italian Renaissance. I did not pursue that career, however, because I quickly became disillusioned with trendy teaching methods.

Before becoming a published author in 1989, I was in Civil Service management, then a housewife and mother. From 1991 to 1997, while researching and writing books, I ran my own school for children with learning difficulties, before taking up writing full-time.

I have been interested in history since the age of fourteen, when I read my first adult novel, the rather lurid Henry's Golden Queen, by Lozania Prole, about Katherine of Aragon. I was so enthralled by it that I dashed off to read real history books to find out the truth behind what I had read, and thus my passion for history was born. By the time I was fifteen, I had written a three-volume reference work on the Tudor dynasty, a biography of Anne Boleyn based partly on contemporary sources, and several historical plays; I had also started work on the research that would one day take form as my first published book, Britain's Royal Families.

During the early 1970s, I wrote historical novels and the original version of my second published book, The Six Wives of Henry VIII - 1024 pages long, and single-spaced - and had it rejected on the grounds that there was a world paper shortage! I also researched the lives of all the mediaeval Queens of England, research I have since drawn on for several of my books.

After suffering several rejections, and then finding a fantastic literary agent, whose client I am fortunate to remain to this day, I finally found a publisher - the Bodley Head - in 1988. Later, that imprint was taken over by Random House, at which point I was transferred to Jonathan Cape, my present U.K. publisher. I've been published in the U.S.A. by Ballantine (Ran-dom House) and Grove Weidenfeld/Grove Atlantic, in Canada by McLelland and Stewart, and by numerous publishers all over the world, with my books having been translated into French, Spanish, Korean, Czech, Turkish, Russian, Polish, Hungarian, Chinese and Italian, to name a few! To date (2018), I have published twenty-six titles, and have seven more on contract.

In 2006, I published my first novel, Innocent Traitor, for Hutchinson, another imprint of Random House; this was published by Ballantine in the U.S.A. in 2007. Since then, I have published seven more novels. In 2014 I was delighted to sign a contract with Headline for six novels on the wives of Henry VIII. I have been fortunate throughout in having the support of wonderful publishers and editorial teams on both sides of the Atlantic. I was elected a Fellow of the Royal Society of Arts in 2003 (I resigned in 2016) and made an honourary life patron of Historic Royal Palaces. I`m still pinching myself to make sure that I`m not dreaming it all!

As a non-fiction author, I write 'popular' history. The term has sometimes been used in a derogatory sense by a few people who should know better because all historians use the same sources. History is not the sole preserve of academics, although I have the utmost respect for historians who undertake new research and contribute something new to our knowledge. History belongs to us all, and it can be accessed by us all. And if writing it in a way that is accessible and entertaining, as well as conscientiously researched, can be described as popular, then, yes, I am a popular historian, and am proud and happy to be one.

History is full of wonderful stories and amazing characters. I feel very privileged to be able to bring them to life in both my non-fiction books and my novels. In both cases, I feel that an author has a responsibility to be as true to the facts as is possible. And in an age in which history is increasingly perceived to be 'dumbed down' in schools, on television, and on film, we can all learn from a study of the past. We can discover more about ourselves and our own civilisation.

From my heart, I should like to thank those of you who have bought my books, borrowed them from libraries, attended my events, or written to me. I do so appreciate your support and encouragement, your creative comments, and also the occasional criticisms, which

I do take very seriously, and which - I hope - help me to become a better writer. Thanks are also due to everyone who has sent me information, photographs, and ideas for forthcoming books, and to those who just wrote and said how much they enjoyed the ones I'd already written. I was so touched that you`d taken the trouble to write and tell me so.

I am delighted to be a Fellow of the Royal Society of Arts, an honourary Life Patron of Historic Royal Palaces, and Patron of the Barnet Medieval Festival, Red Rose Chain, and Anne of Cleves' House, Lewes.

Alison Weir

http://www.alisonweir.org.uk/

ON WRITING HISTORICAL FICTION WITH BEST-SELLING AUTHOR,

ALISON WEIR

When writing a historical novel you can develop ideas and themes that have no place in a history book, but which - based on sound research and educated guesses - help to illuminate the story and explain motives and actions. A historian uses such inventiveness at their peril - but a novelist has the power to get inside the subject`s head and actually be him/her, and that can afford insights that would not be permissable to a historian, and yet can have a legitimate value of their own. A historian has to work within the strict constraints imposed by the source material and credible speculation. A novelist, however, is able to use imagination to fill in the gaps, although I strongly feel that what is invented must be credible within the context of what is known about the subject.

While it is liberating to be able to use your imagination, you cannot indulge in flights of fancy. That sells short both those who know nothing about the subject and those who know a great deal. Many people care that what they are reading in a historical novel is close to the truth, given a little dramatic licence. Because lots of people — myself included — first come to history through historical novels, and many rely on the novelist to tell it as it was, and to set the story within an authentic background, with authentic detail. Thus you have a great responsibility towards your readers. You want them to trust you, so adhere to the facts where they exist and use your informed imagination where they don't. History does not always record people's

motives, emotions and reactions, or the intimate details of their relationships or their love lives, so there is plenty of scope for invention there.

The setting should be authentic. Some historical novels fall down because the author has not done enough background research. They know the story superficially, but they don't know the period and they have a simplistic view of the characters. So do all the research you can, not only on your charaters but on the historical context and the world they inhabit.

How far dare you make things up or manipulate the facts in a novel about a real historical personage? My feeling is that you should have some historical evidence, however flimsy, on which to base tha aspect of the plot. For a historian, such evidence may not be convincing, but it might be a gift to a novelist. For example, in The Other Boleyn Girl, Philippa Gregory has Anne Boleyn, desperate to have a son, contemplating committing incest with her brother because he is the only man who can safely be relied upon not to betray their intimacy to others. The historical Anne was charged with incest in the indictment drawn up against her, and while other evidence strongly suggests that these were trumped-up charges, a novelist may use them as the basis of a good plot. I have no argument with that. Again, the issue of Elizabeth I`s much-vaunted virginity has been endlessly debated by scholars, so in my view, it is quite legitimate for novelists such as Susan Kay in Legacy and Robin Maxwell in The Queen`s Bastard to depict the Queen having a physical relationship with the Earl of Leicester. I myself took a similar liberty, going against what I believe as a historian, in my second novel, The Lady Elizabeth. What I wrote there was based purely on unreliable gossip and coincidental dates but had this contemporary evidence not existed, I would not have ventured so far. But it does exist, and even though, as a historian, I would discount it, as a novelist, I have the freedom to ask, what if?

Always explain what is fact and what is fiction in an Author`s Note at the end of each book. If the book is largely fictional, say so. It matters when you are writing about real people and events because many people accept historical fiction as fact. The major challenge to any author embarking on a historical novel is the use of language. There are tough choices, and you will never please everyone. You could adopt pseudo-Tudor speak and alienate your readers with words and phrases such as `prithee` or `hey nonny nonny`; or you could go to the other extreme, as Suzannah Dunn does in her wonderful book, The Queen of Subtle-

ties, where she has Anne Boleyn calling her father `Dad`. Or you could use modern, plain speech to the same effect.

Having spent many years studying Tudor sources, I'm familiar with the idioms of language in use then - although we can never know how people actually spoke, only how their words were written down, which may not be the same thing. Wherever possible, I use my characters' own historical quotes, or the quotes of others, lifting them from historical sources, but modernising them slightly so that they do not stand out awkwardly in modern text. In order to appeal to as wide - and as young - an audience as possible, I confess to using a few modern idioms where I think they sound better than their Tudor equivalent, even if they are anachronistic. But it's impossible to please everyone: while one reviewer deplored the anachronistic language in my first novel, another said I had got it just right!

Writing in the first person affords a narrower view, u less you use several narrators, as I did in that book. The challenge there is to differentiate the voices. The present tense makes the story more immediate. In my later no els, I have used the past tense and the third person, which allows for greater versatility in telling the story. Above all, SHOW rather than TELL. The reader has to see things happening.

NEW FROM ALISON WEIR - "THE KING'S PLEASURE" (USA) - "HENRY VIII: THE HEART & THE CROWN (UK) RELEASING MAY 2023

In grand royal palaces, Prince Harry grows up dreaming of knights and chivalry — and the golden age of kings that awaits his older brother. But Arthur's untimely death sees Harry crowned King Henry of England. As his power and influence extends, so commences, a lifelong battle between head and heart, love and duty. Henry rules by divine right, yet his prayers for a son go unanswered. The future of his great dynasty depends on an heir. And the crown weighs heavy on a king with all but his one true desire.

Alison Weir's most ambitious Tudor novel yet reveals the captivating story of a man who was by turns brilliant, romantic, and ruthless: the King who changed England forever.

"After writing the Six Tudor Queens series of novels on the wives of Henry VIII, all written from each queen's point of view, I thought it would be interesting to give Henry himself a voice in fiction. The result is this novel, Henry VIII: The Heart and the Crown, which imagines the story of his life as he saw it. My aim was to explore not only his relationships with his wives from a very different viewpoint, but also his interactions with the men who dominated his reign: Cardinal Wolsey, Thomas Cromwell, Thomas Cranmer and a host of others who were close to the King. I also wanted to show what made Henry the man he later became, whom some perceive as a tyrant or even a monster; my aim was to draw a more balanced portrait, and to analyse and understand Henry's complex character.

So meet Harry, golden prince and legendary king, the product of a fractured childhood and later a victim of a

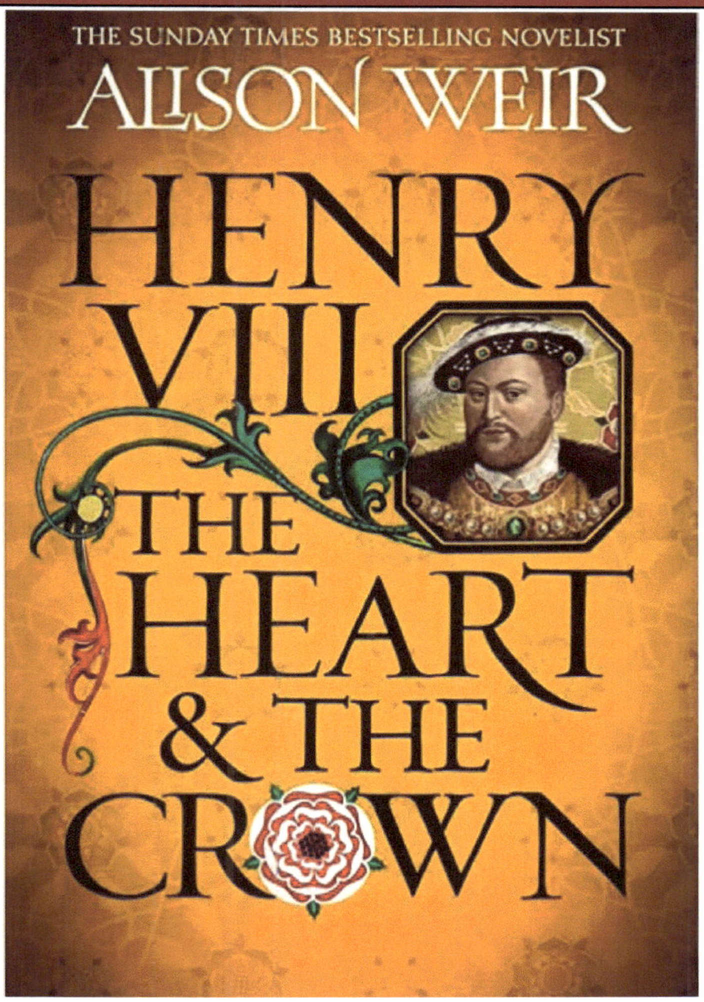

cruel fate that denies him the heirs he needs to secure the succession of the Tudor dynasty. The book begins when he is eleven years old and has been dealt the most painful blow of all. It follows him through his youth and reign, taking an epic journey through forty-four years of one of the most turbulent periods in history — as seen by England's most famous, or (for some) notorious, King.

It's a riveting tale, but ultimately a poignant one, and my hope is that readers will be left with a more sympathetic — and empathetic — view of a man who is all too often portrayed as a caricature of his true self."

UK: HB HEADLINE 2023 (ABOVE)
USA: HB BALLANTINE 2023 (LEFT)

Visit Alison's website to learn more about this book and more, plus click on events to see where she is scheduled for readings or signings.
www.alisonweir.org.uk

THE SECRETIVE WORLD OF ELIZABETHAN MAIDS OF HONOUR

TONY RICHES

Historical fiction author Tony Riches explores the lives of the women who served Queen Elizabeth Ist.

Elizabethan Maids of Honour were a fascinating group of women who witnessed some of the most important events of the time, and helped shape the culture and society of the Elizabethan era. England experienced great change as a more secular culture replaced the religious and political turmoil of the Middle Ages. Women played a more active role in society, and the position of Maid of Honour became one of the most coveted positions for young women of the nobility.

Maids of Honour were usually between sixteen and eighteen years old, and were supposed to be maidens, meaning they could not be married. The queen liked to surround herself with these young women, and ruled over them with absolute authority. Chosen for their beauty, intelligence, and social skills, Maids of Honour were expected to be accomplished in music, dancing, and conversation.

They also had to be discreet and loyal, as they were entrusted with sensitive information. The life of a Maid of Honour was one of privilege, and their prestigious position offered opportunities for advancement. The role became the ultimate preparation for a career at court, and many Maids of Honour went on to marry well and become ladies-in-waiting to the queen.

There were around a dozen Maids of Honour, and new candidates waited for their chance when one left to marry — or was banished in disgrace. Their main duties were to run errands for the queen and more senior ladies, carrying messages and entertaining, with singing and dancing, as well as playing musical instruments.

There is a surprising lack of detail about the ladies in waiting to Queen Elizabeth I, so we must deduce who did what, and when, from source documents such as lists of New Year gifts, letters and court records. There was also regular promotion, usually after marriage, from Maids of Honour to Ladies and Gentlewomen of the Privy Chamber and Ladies of the Bedchamber — and demotion, depending who was out of favour.

Maids of Honour were held to higher standards than other women in society. The queen imposed strict rules of conduct, and their behaviour was under the constant scrutiny of the court. They were often at the centre of court life, expected to attend court functions, participate in the queen's entertainments, and to attend the queen at all times of the day and night.

When not on a royal progress, they lived in the queen's household in the 'maiden's chambers'. Often privy to the queen's private thoughts and feelings, the most trusted were used as messengers. Maids of Honour were expected to maintain absolute discretion, as any indiscretion could have serious consequences.

Long periods when there was little to do meant their chambers became a place of gossip, secrets and intrigue, although they soon learned how dangerous speculation about the queen could be. Much of the gossip was about the game of courtly love, encouraged by gentlemen courtiers, who risked imprisonment or banishment from court by breaking the queen's rules.

Surprisingly, Maids of Honour also passed the long hours of 'waiting' by gambling at endless games of cards, dice, and backgammon. They were often invited to play against the queen, although she was a poor loser. Court records suggest the queen was happiest taking the r money — and seemed unconcerned they might deliberately allow her to win.

Not all Maids of Honour were noble. Mistress Margaret Radcliffe became a Maid of Honour at court in 1561 at the age of eleven, when her father, Member of Parliament Humphrey Radcliffe, presented her to the queen as a New Year's Day gift. Margaret Radcliffe modelled her life on that of the queen, and never married or retired, remaining in post for forty-two years, until Queen Elizabeth died in 1603.

The queen worried about Catholic plots, and like a spider at the centre of a web, relied on her spymaster, Francis Walsingham's, network of informers. It is likely she used her loyal maids, such as Mistress Radcliffe, to keep her informed about the gossip at court. It's also probable that she asked her Maids of Honour to act as spies and informers, and encourage her courtiers to share frank opinions and private views on politics and religion.

Maids of Honour needed the queen's permission to marry, yet she usually refused. One of the most famous Maids of Honour to fall foul of this was Lettice Knollys, daughter of Francis Knollys and Catherine Carey, the daughter of Anne Boleyn's sister, Mary. Banished from court for life after the queen learned of her illegal marriage to Robert Dudley, Lettice raised her own daughters, Penelope and Dorothy, both goddaughter's of the queen, to be Maids of Honour.

As well as being tutored in French, Latin and Spanish, they learned to dance, sing and play the lute from a young age. They were sent to the King's House in York to complete their education and prepare for life at court under the guardianship of their stepfather Robert Dudley's sister, Katherine Hastings, Countess of Huntingdon.

ELIZABETH I'S
MAIDS OF HONOUR

Nicolas Hilliard portrait of Queen Elizabeth I

Upper middle:

Anne Vavasour

Upper right:

Margaret Radcliffe

Lower middle left:

Mary Fitton

Lower middle right:

Dorothy and Penelope Devereux

Images from Wikipedia

Countess Katherine used her influence at court to 'put her highness in mind of these young ladies'. Penelope, as the eldest, was invited to court at the age of eighteen in January 1581, a year of festivities to celebrate the queen's engagement to the young Duke of Anjou. One of her first royal outings was to accompany the queen to a banquet aboard Francis Drake's ship, the Golden Hinde, to celebrate his circumnavigation of the world, and witnessed him being knighted by the French ambassador.

She soon became a favourite of the queen, in spite of her mother, and was described as the most beautiful of all the queen's ladies. She attracted the attention of the soldier poet, Philip Sidney, and was the inspiration for 'Stella' in his famous sonnet sequence, Astrophel and Stella., but she'd seen what happened to Maids of Honour who broke the queen's strict rules, and took care not to cause any scandal.

Others were less careful. Soon after Penelope's arrival at court, another Maid of Honour, Anne Vavasour, gave birth to an illegitimate son in the maiden's chamber. Despite best efforts, it proved impossible to keep the birth secret, and both Anne and her lover, Edward de Vere, Earl of Oxford, were locked up in the Tower of London on the orders of the Queen.

Unfortunately for Penelope, her stepfather, Robert Dudley, forgiven and back at court, persuaded the queen to consent to her betrothal to a wealthy puritan businessman, Lord Robert Rich. Penelope had no say in the matter, as refusal after the queen had given permission was not an option. She was condemned to an unhappy marriage to a man she detested - and had to leave the excitement of court for his remote and austere mansion in the country.

Penelope's younger sister Dorothy made the mistake of marrying Thomas Perrot without the queen's permission, Thomas was imprisoned in the Fleet, and Dorothy was banished from court. Even when her brother Robert, Earl of Essex became the queen's favourite he was unable to persuade her to relent until Thomas died, and Dorothy returned to court to also become a royal favourite.

In the summer of 1592, Elizabeth's Captain of the Guard, Walter Raleigh, and one of her Maids of Honour, Bess Throckmorton, were imprisoned in the Tower after the queen learned of their clandestine marriage and the birth of a son. Her penalty in their case was among the most severe. Bess Throckmorton remained incarcerated in the Tower until the end of the year. Her infant son died, and she was permanently excluded from the court.

Mary Fitton became a Maid of Honour to Queen Elizabeth in 1595. After a scandalous affair with William Herbert, later Earl of Pembroke, Mary Fitton became pregnant, and in March 1601 gave birth to a baby boy who died soon after. William Herbert was sent to the Fleet Prison after admitting paternity but refusing to marry his mistress, and Mary was banished from court.

Maids of Honour played an important role in the queen's life as her companions, her confidantes, informers and her friends. They lived under the constant threat of banishment, yet helped to shape Queen Elizabeth's public image and make her reign one of the most successful in English history.

# # #

"The cause of your summons hither at this time is to inform you that it hath pleased Almighty God to call to his own our sovereign lady, Queen Mary. Even as heavy and grievous as this news is to us, so too have we cause to rejoice; for in his infinite mercy God hath provided us with a true and lawful inheritrix to the crown of This Mighty Realm of England. I speak of Her Grace, Elizabeth, our princess, second daughter to our late sovereign, he of noble memory, King Henry, the Eighth of that name, in our line of esteemed and illustrious rulers, and sister of our late queen. Her Grace's lawful right and title to the crown, thanks be to God, we need not doubt."

-Nicholas Heath, Archbishop of York and Lord Chancellor of England, from his address to Parliament on Elizabeth's ascension to the throne of England

THIS MIGHTY REALM

QUEEN ELIZABETH I: THE TRIUMPHANT STORY OF ENGLAND'S GREATEST MONARCH

BONNY G. SMITH

Elizabeth Tudor was a thoroughly English queen, having been born of no foreign princess, as had her sister Mary, who was half Spanish. Elizabeth was a master propagandist; as queen regnant, only the second in English history, she used her considerable skills to turn to her advantage any state of affairs that would help to support her dubious position. She was a reigning monarch who was female, Protestant in a world still dominated by Roman Catholicism, and whom some considered illegitimate and unfit to rule.

Against all odds, Elizabeth I of England not only survived, she thrived; her reign is remembered as a golden era of peace and prosperity. She was the first English monarch to give her name to an age. The enigma that was Elizabeth still inspires awe in us almost five hundred years later. But who was Queen Elizabeth Tudor, and how did she overcome such overwhelming disadvantages to become a legend in her own time? This short biography of a truly extraordinary woman and queen attempts to answer these questions.

Image from Shutterstock

A Royal Birth

On a golden September Sunday in the late summer of 1533, Queen Anne Boleyn went into labor at the Palace of Placentia, also known as Greenwich Palace. The choice of venue for the queen's royal 'confinement' was no accident; Katharine of Aragon had given birth to Mary there, and Greenwich was also the birthplace of Elizabeth's father, King Henry VIII, and was his favorite amongst his array of royal castles and palaces. England, indeed, all of Christendom, held its collective breath in anticipation of the outcome of this controversial royal birth. Already there was a deep fissure, not only in England, but on the European continent as well, between the Old Religion and the fledgling Protestant faction, for which King Henry VIII had become an unwitting hero with his audacious break from the Roman Catholic Church.

So must it not have been with joyful anticipation that Anne, who labored, and Henry, who fretted and impatiently bided his time, waited for this royal child to come into the world? Unfortunately, no. By the time Henry was finally able to marry the woman he had turned the world upside down to possess, he had already begun to tire of her. Anne also showed signs of the severe strain of years of nerve-racking waiting to learn what her ultimate fate was to be. At this point, Anne knew that her future hung by a slender thread: she must deliver the longed-for son and heir, or face a very uncertain future as queen.

Ironically, no one expected what actually happened, except perhaps Anne's implacable enemies; for when the labor was done and the child slipped at last into the world, it was not the expected boy, but a girl. Many dramatizations of Henry's reaction to this embarrassing disaster have been offered, but we do have an eyewitness account from Eustace Chapuys, the Imperial ambassador to England. He reported to the Holy Roman Emperor, Charles V, that both the king and queen manifested 'great disappointment' at the child's sex. Anyone acquainted with the legendary Tudor temper may only wonder at the form this 'great disappointment' actually took; it was likely unpleasant enough to send all the astrologers, sooth-sayers, prognosticators, wise-women, court physicians and winking midwives scurrying to safety regarding their erroneous predictions of a male birth.

The celebratory jousts and most of the elaborate ceremonials planned to welcome the birth of a prince were hurriedly cancelled; but at least the child was vouchsafed the royal christening that had been so joyfully planned for her brother. She was named Elizabeth, for both of her grandmothers.

SIDEBAR: 'The old duchess of Norfolk bare the child [to the font] in a mantle of purple velvet…'

A Fraught Childhood

For the first two and a half years of her life, Elizabeth enjoyed the status of royal princess and heir to the throne. The first Act of Succession decreed that Elizabeth's half-sister, Princess Mary, was illegitimate, and named Elizabeth as her father's heir. To add further to Mary's woes, she was banished from court to wait upon her infant sister at the Royal Palace of Hatfield, in Hertfordshire, and was stripped of her title of princess.

By the time Elizabeth was not quite three years old, King Henry had grown impatient with Anne Boleyn's biting personality and failures to produce the son and heir that he so desperately needed. Anne would be judiciously murdered before the entire Christian world after a sensational trial that saw the hapless queen accused of adultery with five men, including her own brother. (Henry never did anything by halves).

It is likely that Anne's death had little impact upon Elizabeth at the time; she was very young and, in accordance with the practice of the day, was being reared by her governess, Lady Bryan, far from court in Hertfordshire. Although Anne would have visited her daughter from time to

Image from Public Domain

time, they would not have spent much time together; Elizabeth likely saw little of her mother.

With Anne Boleyn's fall from grace, Elizabeth in her turn would be branded a bastard, and have her title of princess revoked by her father. A precocious child, Elizabeth recognized immediately the difference this made in her status and treatment; it is recorded that she remarked to Lady Bryan, 'How now! How haps it that yesterday my Lady Princess, and today but my Lady Elizabeth?' She and her elder sister, Lady Mary, seventeen years her senior, were now in the same miserable boat.

Becoming Elizabeth

We do not know exactly when, or how, Elizabeth learned the story of her mother's dark fate. But the revelation must have been a watershed moment that set her path for the rest of her life. It is documented that Elizabeth, at the tender age of eight years, told her childhood friend, Robert Dudley, that she would never marry.

Elizabeth likely went in awe of her larger-than-life father; perhaps she grew to have a desire to emulate him. If such was her aim, one must agree that she hit the mark. But as an impressionable child and an amazingly astute adolescent, she would have heard what happened to her half-sister Mary's mother; she now knew what her father had done to her own mother; she had witnessed Jane Seymour, of whom she was quite fond, endure a pregnancy fraught with worry about the sex of the child, only to die a long and painful death after bearing Henry the son he had shed gallons of blood to get; she had seen Anne of Cleves' heartbreak at being cruelly thrust aside; she would never recover from what she had watched her cousin, Katherine Howard, go through. Katherine's fate was truly frightening, and a cruel reminder of what her mother had suffered. These real-life experiences would serve as a cautionary tale to convince Elizabeth that marriage, for women, was a dangerous proposition, and was to be avoided at all costs.

'How now! How haps it that yesterday my Lady Princess, and today but my Lady Elizabeth?'

The Dangerous Years

When King Henry died in 1547, Elizabeth was only 13. Prince Edward, at nine years of age, was now king. Mary, who was her siblings' elder by so many years, had been like a mother to them, during the time when both princesses were relegated to comparative obscurity with the birth of a son and heir. This was especially true where Elizabeth was concerned; Mary's privy purse expenses reveal that she often provided her little sister with spending money, small gifts, and new clothes over those years.

They were all orphans now, but Elizabeth and Edward, being nearer in age, and sharing a religion, clung to each other and cried. Both were resident at Elsyng Palace at the time of their father's death, where Elizabeth shared her brother's fine tutors. Elizabeth never questioned that she must give way to her brother; she had, at that time, no reason to expect ever to be queen. Edward was now king; he would marry and have children, and his line would succeed to the throne.

King Henry was married to his sixth wife, Catherine Parr, at the time of his death. Mary was an adult, but Elizabeth was not, and she went to live with Catherine, now Queen Dowager, who by all accounts was an excellent stepmother to the royal children. Catherine married her old love, Thomas Seymour, shortly after Henry's death. But unbeknownst to her, she was actually his third choice. The Lord High Admiral had tried to wed Princess Mary, who refused him with great contempt for the fortune hunter he was. Now, even though he was married to Catherine, Seymour began to aggressively pursue Elizabeth. His motive was his burning desire to oust from power his brother, Edward Seymour, Duke of Somerset, who had effectively seized control of the realm as Lord Protector of England for their underage nephew, now King Edward VI.

Seymour's attentions flattered the teenage Elizabeth, whose passage from childhood to womanhood was occurring just at that time. At first Catherine, now heavily pregnant, went along with the jollity, even helping Seymour cut Elizabeth's mourning gown to pieces in the garden at Catherine's Chelsea home, amidst gales of laughter. But these antics only served to fuel a dangerous fire. It seems inevitable that Catherine would walk in on her husband and her step-daughter in a compromising position. Elizabeth was immediately packed off to Cheshunt, but the damage was done. After a difficult labor, Catherine delivered a daughter to Thomas Seymour. Less than a week later, she died.

But Thomas did not mourn for long; now single again, the Lord High Admiral, envious of his brother's power as Lord Protector, conceived a plot to abduct the boy king, marry him to Lady Jane Grey, marry Elizabeth himself, oust his brother, and seize power. This hare-brained scheme was destined for failure; unfortunately, Elizabeth was also implicated. Seymour was arrested and sent to the Tower, along with Elizabeth's governess, Kat Ashley, and others of the princess's household.

This was a nightmare time for the fifteen-year-old Elizabeth. She was closely questioned to determine her guilt in Seymour's conspiracy, but as her chief interrogator lamented, 'She hath a very good wit, and nothing is got of her but by great policy'. As young as she was, Elizabeth walked the wire successfully; she was exonerated, along with her hapless servants. However, Thomas Seymour went to the block for his folly. We will never know Elizabeth's true feelings, but when informed of the Lord High Admiral's death on the block, she deadpanned that 'This day died a man of great wit, but very little judgment'. Disgraced and with her reputation in tatters, Elizabeth's detractors quipped that what else could one expect from the daughter of Anne Boleyn? And yet Elizabeth had learnt a valuable lesson, and one that would stand her in good stead when her talent for confounding her enemies would be needed once more; for this was not the last time the young princess would face down death.

With the downfall of the Seymours, another rose to prominence as Lord Protector. John Dudley, having made himself indispensable to the boy king, hatched a plot to ensure that his protégé would be succeeded not by his Catholic sister, Mary, but by their Protestant cousin, Lady Jane Grey; Lady Jane was the grandniece of Henry VIII. Dudley created himself Duke of Northumberland, and married Jane to his son Guildford, who, incidentally, was the younger brother of Elizabeth's lifelong friend and paramour, Robert Dudley. When King Edward VI died at age fifteen of what appears to have been sepsis, Dudley seized the throne in Jane's name. But Mary, the granddaughter of the redoubtable warrior queen, Isabella of Castile, was not to be so lightly pushed aside. She raised an army, and took back her throne. But Mary was unconvinced that Elizabeth had not also cast a covetous eye on her crown. Mary, therefore, remained very wary of her half-sister.

Very much aware of being a Catholic monarch in what had developed into a Protestant state since her father's death more than a decade before, Mary was suspicious of her Protestant sister. When Sir Thomas Wyatt, coincidentally the son of one of Anne Boleyn's great admirers, learned that Queen Mary was planning to marry into Spain, he conceived a plot to depose Mary and put Elizabeth on the throne. Once again, even though frightened out of her wits at being placed in the dreaded Tower of London and suspected of treachery against her sister, Elizabeth managed to navigate the dangerous waters of treason. She emerged from yet another frightening ordeal with her head still on her shoulders.

Queen at Last

In November 1558, Elizabeth's half-sister, Queen Mary, died without issue at the age of forty-two. There was no one else at that point; the throne belonged, indisputably, to Elizabeth. Or did it? The majority of those in Christendom were still Catholic, and in their estimation, it was not the Protestant Elizabeth Tudor who was the rightful queen of England, but Mary of Scotland.

Queen of Scotland practically from birth, Mary Stuart was the granddaughter of Margaret Tudor, Henry VIII's elder sister, making her Elizabeth's first cousin, once removed. Mary was married to the Dauphin François, and poised someday to ascend the throne of France as Queen Consort. King Henri II and Mary's powerful Guise relations saw Mary's claim to the throne of England by right of birth,

and incidentally, because Elizabeth was considered illegitimate in Catholic circles, as a tremendous opportunity to expand and consolidate their power in Europe. Scotland already was, and England would then become, mere satellites of powerful France.

Because of Mary Stuart's bold claim to Elizabeth's crown (the Queen of Scots even had the temerity to display the royal arms of England), a harsh spotlight shone on Elizabeth for almost her entire reign. That is, until 1587 when, after almost twenty years under house arrest in England, Elizabeth reluctantly signed Mary's death warrant, and the Scottish queen was beheaded at Fotheringay Castle. Mary had made a valiant effort to rule Protestant Scotland as a Catholic monarch, but for many reasons, she failed, and fled to England and Elizabeth for help regaining her lost kingdom. Mary's naïveté was no match for Elizabeth's realpolitik; after almost two decades of looking over her shoulder, Elizabeth finally agreed with her ministers that Mary had to go if the realm was ever to be truly safe.

All the Queen's Men

The Virgin Queen boasted scores of sycophantic men who sang her praises, and chief amongst these was

Robert Dudley, her great childhood friend. Along with Elizabeth's tarnished reputation from her teenage years, the fact that she was Anne Boleyn's daughter, the fact that Dudley was a married man, and that she was a reigning queen who could, pretty much, do as she pleased, there were many who regarded the so-called 'Virgin Queen' with a raised eyebrow and a gimlet eye. Then when Robert's wife died in mysterious circumstances, a scandal of epic proportions broke out. Dudley was accused of murder in order to free himself for marriage with the queen. We will never know the truth of all this,

but if Elizabeth was considering marrying Dudley, who was, after all, the true love of her life, this sordid episode scotched any such plans.

There were many other suitors over the years; Christopher Hatton would never marry, that he might devote himself to his queen in Courtly Love; Thomas Heneage was another life-long admirer, along with Edward Courtenay, Earl of Devon. Francis Drake and Walter Raleigh also jealously sought the queen's favor. But perhaps the most famous of Elizabeth's beaux was François, the duc du Alençon.

Elizabeth was in her forties when she was courted by this French prince, the youngest son of Catherine de'Medici; he was about 24. This was very much a last chance for the aging queen, but Elizabeth now had her sister Mary's miserable example of a failed marriage with Philip of Spain to add to her repertoire of reasons not to marry; she could add to this dismal list Mary Stuart's two disastrous marriages in Henry, Lord Darnley, and the Earl of Bothwell. Good sense prevailed, and Elizabeth ended the romantic interlude she had enjoyed with a tearful goodbye to her 'frog', as she affectionately called Alençon.

Alençon was not the only foreign prince to seek Elizabeth's hand in marriage. Eric of Sweden threw his crown into the ring, along with several other foreign powers, but alas, to no avail; the Virgin Queen used marriage as a diplomatic bargaining tool, but never with the intention of following through. Elizabeth would share her power with no man.

Probably the most sensational of Elizabeth's men was Robert Devereux, the Earl of Essex. Essex was the son of Elizabeth's cousin, Lettice Knollys, and stepson of Robert Dudley, who had died in 1588. Thirty years her junior, Essex nonetheless made quite a show of romancing his aging sovereign. Great love was professed long and loudly on both sides, but Essex was one of those who simply did not know when to quit; he took shameless advantage of the queen's infatuation on numerous occasions. But when he attempted a military coup to seize her throne, she had little choice but to try him for treason. He was found guilty and beheaded in 1601, two years before Elizabeth died at the age of 69.

In a speech to Parliament, who many times over the years had harangued their queen about the utter necessity of marrying and producing an heir, Elizabeth declared, 'This shall be for me sufficient; that a marble stone shall declare that a Queen, having reigned such and such a time, lived and died a virgin.'

The End of an Era

Perhaps Elizabeth's greatest achievement as queen, at least the best known, was the defeat of the Spanish Armada in the summer of 1588. Certainly, the attempted invasion of England by her former brother-in-law and suitor became the occasion for one of the eloquent Tudor queen's most famous speeches. As the fifty-five-year-old queen reviewed her troops, she declared that: 'I know I have the body but of a weak and feeble woman; but I have the heart and stomach of a king, and a king of England, too!'
With the utter annihilation of the Spanish threat, English pride, as well as its sovereign's prestige, had been given a mighty boost.

Robert Dudley, the Earl of Essex - Image from Wikipedia

> *'This shall be for me sufficient; that a marble stone shall declare that a Queen, having reigned such and such a time, lived and died a virgin.'*

Not long after, Edmund Spenser cast Elizabeth forever in the role of the Faerie Queen in his epic poem. Elizabeth had now actually become that semi-divine being of her long-ago coronation in the guise of Gloriana. Not only had Elizabeth succeeded in overcoming the obstacle of being a female ruler, she had parlayed mere royal power into her own form of episcopacy as Supreme Governor of the Church of England. Many believed England to be the better for it.

Elizabeth's greatest, most enduring achievement was the Elizabethan Religious Settlement. After years of factional strife in England between Catholic and Protestant, a common doctrine was declared, with compromises made to appeal to both sides. There were still dissenters, but unless they were caught plotting the queen's death, they were dealt with in accordance with Elizabeth's famously stated position: 'I have no desire to make windows into men's souls'. Quite a different outlook to Queen Mary's. Simply put, the difference between Elizabeth and her sister was tolerance.

"Spanish Armada" by Loutherbourg == Image from Wikipedia

Elizabeth's religious settlement marked the end of the Protestant Reformation in England; the Church of England developed a national identity that still endures today.

After decades of promoting her image of the Virgin Queen, Elizabeth came to symbolize for some a figure akin to the Virgin Mary; a demi-goddess, anointed of God, a semi-divine being by virtue of her coronation. Elizabeth became almost Christlike in the national psyche, a queen willing to sacrifice herself for the good of her realm; for had she not given up love, marriage, and children, to ensure the peace and prosperity of her kingdom? As Elizabeth herself once said to Parliament, holding up that porcelain-skinned hand with its long, slender fingers, one of which bore her coronation ring, her husband was England, the people, her children.

What became known as the Elizabethan Era saw many other achievements. The queen's patronage of the arts helped yield such genius as the plays of William Shakespeare, and the concomitant Elizabethan theatre; intellectual curiosity and the financing of exploration resulted in the discovery of the rest of the world, something we take for granted, but must have been quite a shock to our brothers of the past; the first poor laws were established, to help the less fortunate. England became a major player in European politics, and this set the stage for the empire that would follow. All this, from a troubled realm that had been bankrupt when it was inherited by a slip of a girl with a tarnished reputation and the twin handicaps of being both female, and illegitimate in the eyes of Catholic Europe.

Good Queen Bess, as her people affectionately referred to her, ruled England for almost forty-five years; indeed, at the time of her death, many had known no other monarch. But there was one thing Elizabeth had not provided for her people; she had no heir of her body. And yet, by her stubborn refusal during her entire reign to name an heir, thereby defusing any real focus for rebellion, Elizabeth had ensured the ongoing peace and prosperity of her realm. On her death bed, she finally named James Stewart, King James VI of Scotland, the son of her cousin and greatest rival, as England's next sovereign. Her final gift to her beloved country was the assurance of a peaceful succession; this was, perhaps, her greatest achievement.

'And though God hath raised me high, yet this I count the glory of my Crown, that I have reigned with your loves.'
'You may have many princes more mighty and wise, yet you never had nor shall have, any that will be more loving.'

– Elizabeth, from her 'Golden Speech' to Parliament 1601

Image from Wikipedia

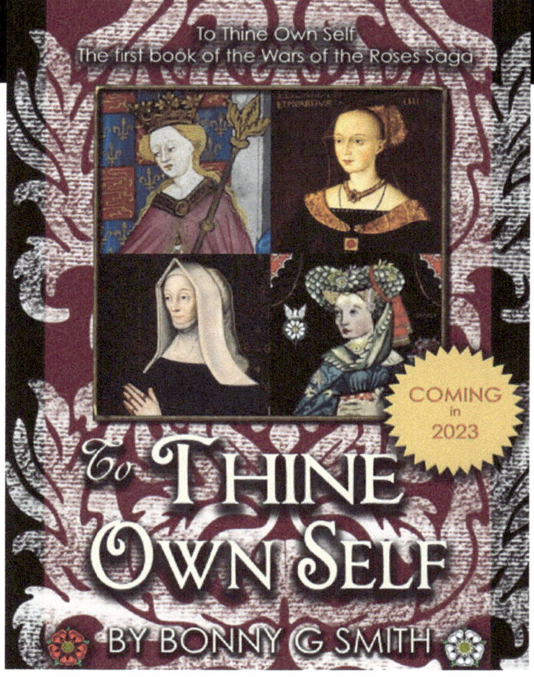

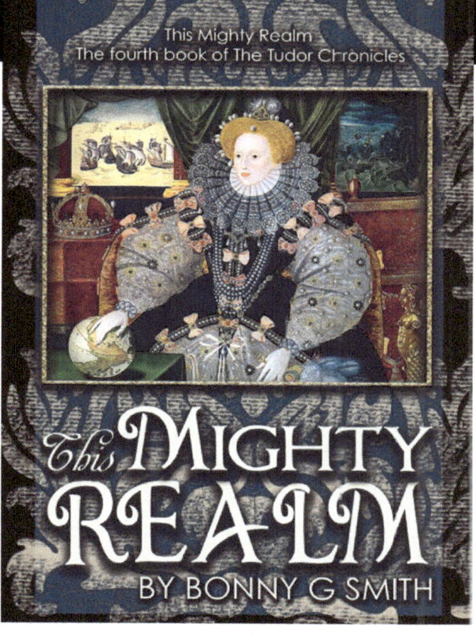

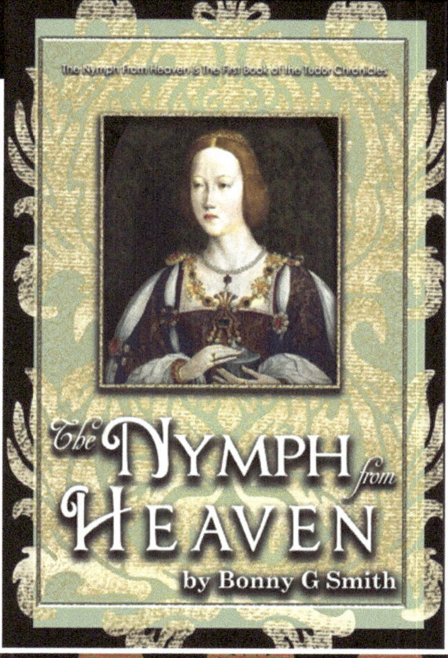

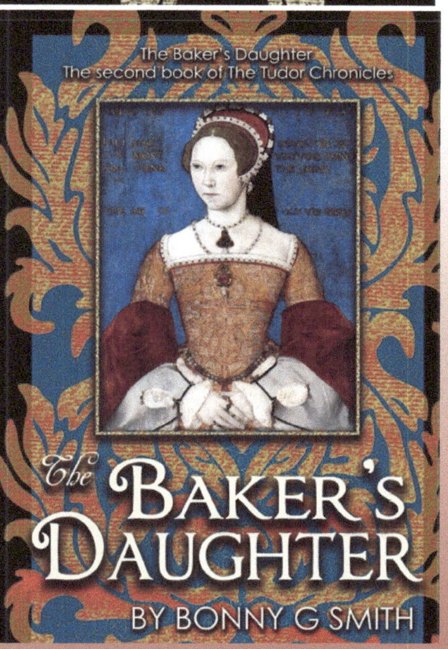

COMING 2023!

**BOOKS
AVAILABLE AT
AMAZON**

www.bonnygsmith.com

BONNY G. SMITH

The Tudor Chronicles

Bonny G Smith enjoyed a career as a Certified Project Manager, working for several major telecommunications corporations. She holds baccalaureate and master's degrees from the University of Maryland. After spending a lifetime reading history, biography and historical fiction, Ms. Smith decided to write her own novels about her favorite era, Tudor England; The Tudor Chronicles consists of five novels, beginning in the early sixteenth century and ending in 1603. Ms. Smith began writing in 2003, and is the author of seven novels and a book of short stories, across four literary genres. She is currently writing a new series, The Wars of the Roses Saga, which will consist of two novels; To Thine Own Self will be published in the fall of 2023. The second book of the series, For Thine is the Kingdom, is currently scheduled for publication in 2026. Ms. Smith lives in Fairfax, Virginia, in the United States of America.

AUTHOR WEB SITE: http://bonnygsmith.com
FACEBOOK: http://facebook.com/authorbonnygsmith/
INSTAGRAM: https://instagram.com/authorbonnygsmith?igshid=YmMyMTA2M2Y=
TWITTER: https://twitter.com/BonnyGSmith2
PINTREST: https://www.pinterest.com/bonny_gsmith/

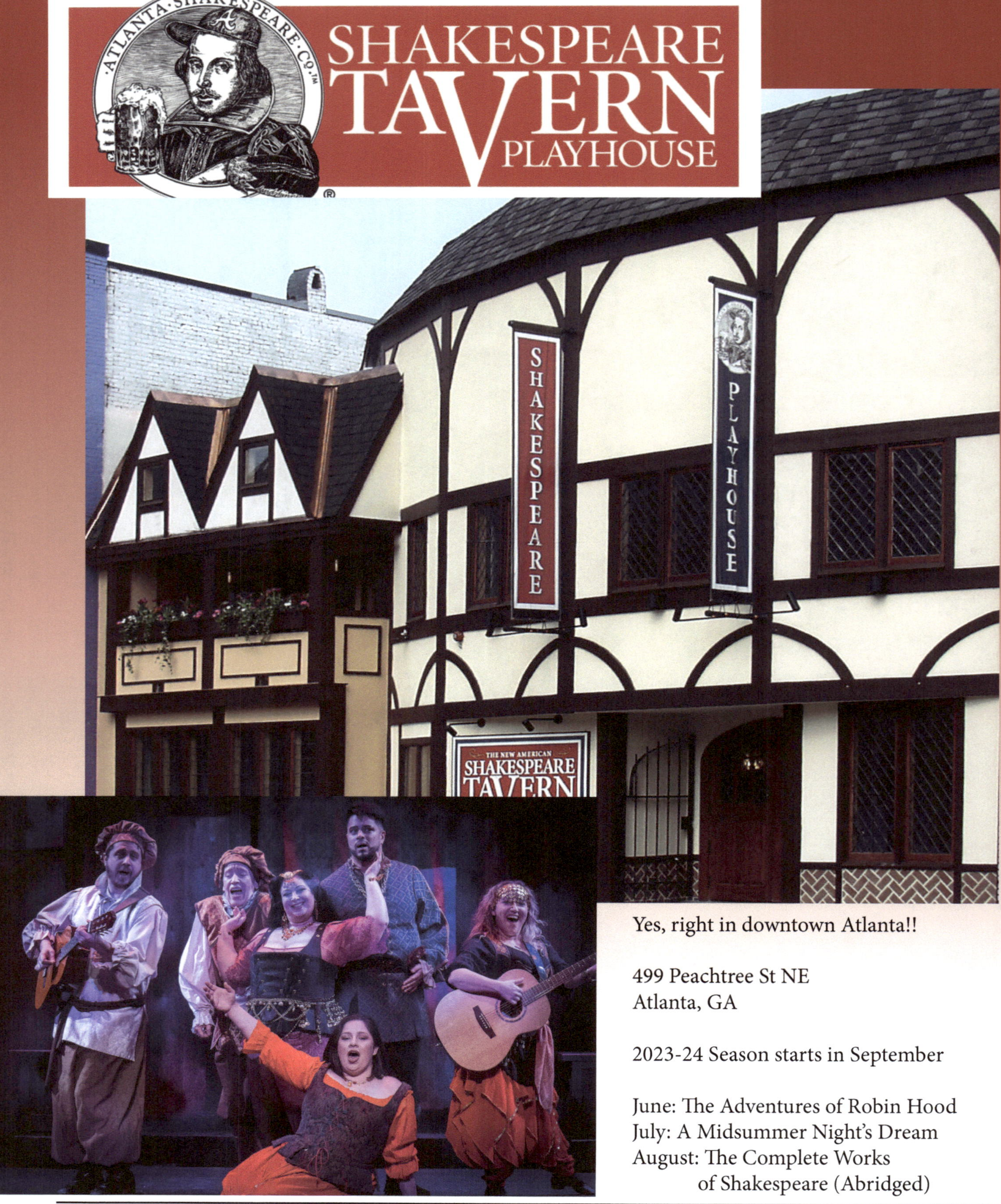

Yes, right in downtown Atlanta!!

499 Peachtree St NE
Atlanta, GA

2023-24 Season starts in September

June: The Adventures of Robin Hood
July: A Midsummer Night's Dream
August: The Complete Works
    of Shakespeare (Abridged)

For a one of a kind experience with some Southern hospitality, enjoy a night out with the Bard.
With each production from the late 80's until 1999, ASC's core aesthetic became a little clearer.

What emerged over time was a company of artists dedicated to a radically pure approach to the text. Each syllable is examined and reexamined for clues as to form, meaning, and original intent. What's more, ASC actors actively embraced the heart and soul of the Elizabethan Theater: the active relationship between actor and audience.

Since the opening of The Shakespeare Tavern® Playhouse on Peachtree Street in 1990, ASC has produced Shakespeare's entire 39 play canon twice, plus over 20 period classics by the likes of Aristophanes, G.B Shaw, Mrs. Aphra Behn, Jean Racine, Christopher Marlowe, Jean Anouilh, Ryunosuke Akutagwa, Niccolo Machiavelli, Albert Camus, Jean Genet, Tennessee Williams, Moliere, Bertolt Brecht, Jean Cocteau, and Thornton Wilder, and a handful of fun musicals such as A Funny Thing Happened on the Way to the Forum, Cabaret and Hamlet, The Musical!.

In 1995 ASC was honored to be the first American company to perform on the stage of Shakespeare's Globe in London, England. - (text from the Shakespeare Tavern website)

*****

As the editor of Historical Times magazine, I've been attending plays at the Shakespeare Tavern since the early 2000s, and love the performances and the food. To watch 'Hamlet' or 'Macbeth' while supping on shepherd's pie with a mug of ale is truly a grand night out. My favorite performances to date have been the yearly production of 'Romeo and Juliet' and the astounding production of 'Doctor Faustus' starring Dikran Tulaine as FAUSTUS (best known for his recurring role in NBC's The Blacklist and guest appearance as Mancea in the final season of The Walking Dead); and Daniel Pettrow as MEPHISTOPHELES, in 2000. I will also never forget a great girl's day out when my besties and I took our teenage daughters to see a matinee of 'Romeo and Juliet' where we squelched our laughter as they giggled and squealed at the handsome young actors in their doublets and tights. Needless to say, we became the 'cool moms' that day!

All in all, while many might tout that to see a Shakespearean play properly, you must see it on-stage at the Globe, or in Stratford, or even anywhere in the UK might suffice, but for the majority of Americans who might never have the opportunity to cross the pond, then this is a great option. The atmosphere is cozy, welcoming, and lends itself to 'groundling' participation for some of the performances.

And the man behind this southern Shakespearean dream is founder, Jeff Watkins, whose greeting words at the beginning of many of the performances sets the mood for the evening. As far as the goals and mission of the American Shakespeare Company, their own words speak more profoundly than any I might conjure... so I give you... their words."
*****

Context: For the people of Shakespeare's Globe, poetry was a living thing brought into existence through the active relationship of actor, audience, and playwright. This is in clear contrast to contemporary dramatic forms where the actor is most often found behind the "fourth wall" (in which the actor pretends that the audience is not present) of 20th Century Theater, or is trapped behind the lens in a film, a medium where true audience interaction is simply not possible. Taking the Elizabethan Theater as a point of beginning, each ASC production is a process calculated to ACTIVATE the relationship between actor, audience, and playwright.

Mission: The Atlanta Shakespeare Company is a quest for a living theater, a theater whose "raison d'être" is the communion of actor and audience through poetry. To foster that communion, we have built the only Original Practice Playhouse®, The Shakespeare Tavern Playhouse, at **499** Peachtree Street in Atlanta, GA. Using this space as a laboratory for the exploration of Elizabethan stagecraft and theatrical techniques, all of our work is guided by a single clarion principle that ASC reveres above all others: the voice of the playwright. This is true whether the company is presenting an original piece, an American classic, or a timeless masterpiece by William Shakespeare. In all cases, each production is a process that begins with the way each play was originally staged in its own time and ends with a modern audience experiencing the play in a manner consistent with its creator's original intent. Thus, when presenting plays by Shakespeare, ASC productions feature hand-made period costumes, all live music and sound effects, thrilling sword fights, and abundant "direct address" to the audience, all of which is orchestrated to assure that the passion and poetry of Shakespeare's genius remains at the heart of the theatrical experience. This is unlike "modern" approaches that routinely update, alter, deconstruct, or otherwise adapt the plays in the service of a 20th Century sensibility. This Core Aesthetic, known as Original Practice, informs and inspires all of our work."
- (Text from the Shakespeare Tavern website at www.shakespearetavern.com)

DEE MARLEY
Historical Times Editor-in-Chief
The Historical Fiction Company CEO

For more information, go to www.shakespearetavern.com

"Pericles")above)

"Merry Wives of Windsor" (left)

Images from Jeff Watkins
The Shakesepeare Tavern
(American Shakespeare Company)

RECREATING THE TUDOR AGE

ELIZABETH KEYSIAN

Have you ever wanted to do something so much, it made you cry? The only times I've experienced it recently is when I've been reading about mouth-watering package holidays around Ancient Greece and the like. However, back when I was freshly out of university and looking for employment, I saw an advert in The Guardian newspaper that grabbed me by the throat and, yes, brought tears to my eyes.

Admittedly, it wasn't a job (I was looking for something in the archaeology/history line at the time), and it wasn't paid. As I discovered later, one had to lay out a bit of money to do it, providing one's own costume and accoutrements. But who could resist the opportunity to pretend to be a Tudor person for a couple of weeks, on a privately owned manor dating back at least as far as the 15th Century, with much of the house and outbuildings untouched by modern advances? Not me, it seemed.

I confess, I already had a grounding in such activities, as I'd belonged to The Sealed Knot, a group who re-enacted battles of the English Civil War. I'd discovered that I could be a different person while dressed in historical costume and dared to do things I'd normally baulk at. But more of that later.

The venue for my new adventure was Kentwell Hall in Suffolk, owned by Patrick Phillips. He'd decided to open up his home to over two hundred willing participants, bringing it back to life as it had been during the Tudor age. The aim would be the education of visiting school parties who were studying the history of the locality, or the Tudor period as a topic. The general public was welcomed at weekends. The income derived from this venture was to be put back into the renovation of the house so it would be safely conserved for posterity, and somewhere for Patrick and Judith to raise their family. Ultimately, the house would be returned to its former glory, as an E-shaped, Elizabethan manor house complete with moat, fish ponds and gardens. Unusually, the original manor house hadn't been demolished to make way for the newer one, so a great deal of work was required to preserve that, too.

What better way to spend the early summer, I thought, than to indulge in a bit of time travel? I was all fired up to head off to Kentwell but then hit a snag; I couldn't find a friend who was able or willing to go with me. Still, as you might be able to tell from my reaction when I saw the advert, I wasn't going to let the lack of comrades stop me. I pushed aside my shyness and anxiety and just went for it.

The Kentwell experience begins with an Open Day. At this event, I learned all the different roles that needed to be filled, met with fellow enthusiasts, discovered what would be required of me, and did some exploring.

Even now, I remember standing in the corridor linking the Tudor kitchen to the Great Hall, with ancient wooden timbers and lath-and-plaster infill just inches from my shoulder. This was history in the flesh! There were no rope barriers separating us, no guides or attendants to tell me what I could, or couldn't do. I felt it a privilege and an honour to be there.

I soon discovered that, during opening hours, I must manage without modern equipment and facilities. It wasn't as bad as it sounds; there were private cellars and lofts where one could grab a cup of coffee or a smoke if one so desired, and the toilets were modern flushing ones. All electrical fittings in the buildings were concealed by swathes of hessian or large bunches of dried herbs and flowers. In the interests of authenticity, the campsite where we slept was out of view of the visitors.

The main Kentwell Event took place over three weeks, prior to the start of the school summer holidays. Each summer, a specific year would be re-enacted, and everyone would need to understand the history, politics, culture, and significance of that year. My first year was 1610, when English culture was still essentially Elizabethan, but would gradually become Jacobean. My second year was 1487, just after the accession of Henry VII; it was very different in style and culture to 1610. Participants were expected to read up on the events and issues of the chosen year; for example, even the lowest of the low would have heard of Henry VIII's Great Matter (when he was attempting to divorce Catherine of Aragon), and they would definitely have known of the Spanish attempt to invade England during the reign of Elizabeth I.

Every participant had to invent a Tudor persona for themselves, and not only become that character but create a backstory, too. So, even though we'd actually just come up the muddy track from the campsite that morning, we claimed to be either "from the village" or to dwell somewhere "on the manor". As well as Tudor roles and believable characters, we adopted names suitable to the era. I went for Avis initially, but in later years, changed to Kate. I still respond to "Kate!" if anyone happens to shout it in my general direction.

Re-enactors at Kentwell Hall - Image provided by Elizabeth Keysian

Authenticity was vital to ensure that the spell of Kentwell wasn't broken. Once visitors had passed through the Time Tunnel, everything they saw, heard, smelled, touched, and tasted had to be recognisably Tudor. The schoolchildren that came during the week were inquisitive and eagle-eyed, as keen to spot anachronisms as we were to conceal them. Participants were advised to stop wearing their watches some weeks before they came to the Event, so there would be no tell-tale white watch marks against otherwise tanned skin. Spectacles were not permitted unless they were handmade in the Tudor style, and even contact lenses were banned; it was considered authentic that some of us wouldn't be able to see where on earth we were going.

One quickly learned the art of deception. When one couldn't block out the modern world completely, one interpreted it in a Tudor fashion. If a visitor asked if they could take a picture, a Kentwell participant would assume they were a painter of portraits, tell them they didn't have time to sit for them and continue about their business. It is rare to find a photo taken by a visitor in which a Kentwelly is looking directly at the camera, or posing.

Entire families participated in the re-enactments, taking their children out of school and dressing them up in appropriate garb. One child, aged around five, was told not to stare at aeroplanes as they flew over because this was the Tudor period, so they hadn't been invented yet. If the boy heard a plane, he was taught to say, "It sounds like thunder." Unfortunately, he didn't get this quite right, and once, when a helicopter flew over, he told the nearby visitors, "Oh! I hear thunder. It sounds like a helicopter."

An important part of becoming a believable Tudor was by wearing costume. Most participants made their own; every garment had to be hand-sewn and made of fabric derived from natural fibres. Only colours that could have come out of a Tudor dye pot were permitted.

Not only did one change one's appearance, one changed the way one spoke. Out went modern expressions such as "okay" and "hi" and in came terms such as "Goodwife" and "Master", and greetings such as "God give you good day." A new kind of language, known as "Tudorese" was born. It was much simpler than Shakespearean English because we didn't want to baffle our visitors, especially since most of them were children. We also behaved according to our place in society, with those participants representing the lower orders bowing or curtsying whenever a member of the gentry appeared.

Many different occupations were available for Kentwell participants. These were referred to as "stations" and were spread around the manor, both outdoors and indoors. The place was run as it might have been back in its heyday, with livestock, stables, its own brewery and bakehouse, hay meadows, herb and vegetable gardens, and formal grounds where the gentlefolk could stroll or play bowls upon the sward.

Kentwell Hall recreations were probably more industrious than a Tudor manor genuinely was. How many Elizabethan manors could boast their own pottery, smithy, chandler (to provide the Main House with beeswax candles), fletcher, glass and bronze-working kilns, limners (painters), soldier's station, players' wagon, and printmaker? There was even a builder's yard, where timber-framed buildings were erected using traditional 16th-century methods. In fact, there were so many different things to do and see that I won't list them all here, but I will go into a little more detail about the stations where I did my own personal bit of re-enacting.

I started out in the stillroom. This station occupied a room in the 15th-century Moat House and was reached by a flight of alarming wooden stairs, from the top of which one could gaze down over the Great Hall of the pre-Elizabethan manor house. The moat itself, filled with frighteningly large carp,

lapped gently against the brick walls of the Moat House. Upstairs in the stillroom, some of the windows were lacking glass, and swallows flew in and nested in the beams above us. Great swathes of herbs hung drying all around the room, and there were dishes of ointments and jars of remedies, as well as a pot full of large garden snails in the middle of the table. When the schoolchildren visited, we offered them cures for their ailments (only the boldest partook), all of which had been carefully vetted by the lady in charge of the stillroom. She was a doctor by profession and knew which ancient cures were safe to employ, and which were better just spoken of.

I had prepared for my role as a "stillroom wench" by studying the 17th-century Culpeper's Herbal, but I didn't have access to the actual plants mentioned therein. Thus, it was a delight to meet them in the flesh, so to speak, and use them in potions. There was also an element of folklore in medieval and Tudor medicine, so we'd advise people to do things like hang dead a dead mouse around their neck to improve a sore throat.

Some of the cures we used were hugely successful; I still swear by the orange sap squeezed from a celandine seedpod for getting rid of warts, and the practice of using a snail on a burn. The snail's slimy trail eases the pain and prevents blistering. I recall one entertaining occasion when the captive snails escaped, and a barefoot stillroom wench trod on one. Many calming remedies were required after that.

After a couple of years in the stillroom, I moved on to the Tudor kitchen. I'd been diagnosed with a sensitivity to dairy products and certain meats, so the only way to make sure I wouldn't be poisoned by our midday pottage was to oversee the making of it. I worked alongside both men and women in the Kentwell kitchen, where we had a fascinating time re-creating whatever historical recipes had survived from the Tudor era.

There may, or may not, have been a modern gas oven hidden away, but we certainly took some tarts and pies to the bakehouse to be cooked and used chafing dishes for smaller quantities of food. The Tudor fireplace held a chimney crane from which we could suspend cauldrons for boiling bag puddings and similar fare over the fire.

The Kentwell cooks decorated all the dishes before the page boys came to take them up to the main hall for gentry lunch. We sometimes had a bit of fun with our betters. I remember serving up "sole" in pastry, which wasn't fish at all, but the sole from somebody's leather shoe. On John the Baptist's day, the gentry table was decorated with a decapitated head on a platter, made from a bread base and covered with marzipan (marchpane). Natural dyes were used for details, such as the hair, eyes, and mouth.

The Main Event in summer wasn't all Kentwell had to offer. Long weekends and Bank Holidays saw Easter and May Day activities available to participants. These were aimed at the general public rather than schools. I attended more than one May Day event, during which I took on the role of "cottager". I spent the day with my invented extended family carding and spinning wool, cooking pottage, singing authentic songs, and making garlands in advance of the May Day celebrations. I also had to deal with the complexities of Tudor pest control (mice), lighting a fire and keeping it going, chopping wood without cutting myself, and learning how to make soft cheese.

The cottage itself consisted of a loft room, where people (mainly me) continually banged their heads on an overhead beam when they went up, a great open room with a hearth by the window, and a separate section to accommodate the livestock. We enjoyed more freedom at the cottage than we did at the Main House. A friend and I invented a game using wooden chopping boards as bats, and an over-baked bread roll from the bakehouse as a ball. I should perhaps add here that all the bread consumed on the manor was made on site, in a genuine 16th-century bread oven. It sometimes took the bakers a little while to get used to using the oven, so the early batches of bread weren't always of the best quality.

Kentwell participants worked hard work and maintained authenticity while the manor was open to the public. As soon as the visitors had gone, the women removed their headgear (coifs are not the most flattering thing to wear) and everyone gathered around the fires to sing, drink, and be merry. There were opportunities to learn new skills, too, such as Tudor dancing, sword-fighting, and archery. I embraced all of these with gusto, although I can't claim to have been the best shot at the butts!

I mentioned earlier that taking on a different persona, and wearing a costume, can change one's behaviour—at least temporarily. I found myself doing things that I would never be bold enough to do in the modern day. One example was accompanying a few friends to collect a swarm of bees clinging to a tree. A basketwork skep had been prepared for them, and the collector covered the end of his sword with honey and dipped it into the swarm. The bees transferred themselves to the sword and were thus transferred to the skep and a lifetime of being cared for by a Tudor-style beekeeper. I realise now that it was somewhat risky for me to be there, but at the time, I was fascinated by the process. I suppose there was always the nearby moat to jump into if one were endangered.

I did, indeed, jump into the moat on one occasion, partly for pleasure and partly because I wanted to do something outrageous. Please don't tell Patrick! It was one of the fish ponds really, empty of fish, and deep enough to swim in. It was a fine summer's morning, and the perfect opportunity to refresh both oneself and one's shift (a simple undergarment for ladies). The gentleman who accompanied us decided to wear nothing at all; I was both shocked and amused, and may, or may not, have used the scene in one of my Elizabethan stories.

The final Brave Thing I did at Kentwell was learning how to breathe fire. I had no idea how it was done until a young lad who went by the Tudor name of Hob handed me some barbecue lighter fluid and a flaming torch and invited me to have a go. I'm not going to give away the secret because I don't want to spoil things for readers, but I did succeed in breathing fire and no one was injured in the process.

The sights, sounds, and smells of my Kentwell experience have stayed with me and the best dreams I have are those in which I return to this impressive, immersive experience. Whenever I smell woodsmoke or bread baking, I think of Kentwell. The scent of lavender, dried rose petals and leather brings it back to me as well. I delved deep into my Kentwell experiences when creating my Trysts and Treachery series of Tudor-era romantic adventures. The first book, Lord of Deceit, uses Kentwell Hall as a model for the invented Selwood Manor.

I wish I could participate in a Kentwell re-creation again, but I'd be blind as a bat without my glasses, and I have too many ailments now to survive so physical an experience. Unless I were to go as a member of the gentry and be waited upon.

I have barely scratched the surface of what goes on during a Kentwell Hall Tudor re-enactment, so if you are ever in Suffolk, England, when there is an Event on, I strongly urge you to visit the place for yourself.
So, good gentles all, our tale is done, and I bid you good day. Or if you're reading this at night time, bene darkmans!

*****

Elizabeth Keysian is an award-winning, USA TODAY bestselling author, who writes historical romances ranging from the medieval to the Victorian era.

Re-enactors at
Kentwell Hall in
Suffolk

Images provided by
Elizabeth Keysian
and Wikipedia

AN ELIZABETHAN PIRATE

OF A DIFFERENT SORT

D. G. MACDOUGALL

The names of Elizabethan-era pirates resound through the centuries: Drake, Gilbert, Grenville, Hawkins, and Raleigh. Queen Elizabeth I of England presided over the so-called Golden Age of Pirates, more-or-less legitimating (and glorifying) the piratical exploits of these gentlemen against England's greatest foe: Spain.

What is less known is that the English themselves were frequent targets of piracy—but from the most unlikely of foes: Scotland. And the greatest Scottish pirate of them all was Rory "The Tartar" MacNeil, chief of the clan MacNeil of Barra. Also called Rory "The Turbulent," his attacks on English shipping would ultimately bring him unwelcome attention from Queen Elizabeth herself—and her cousin, King James VI of Scots.

Barra is the south-most in the chain of islands that make up the Outer or Western Hebrides; for centuries it was simply called the Long Island. The Long Island's most significant human occupiers have been the clans that made it their territory: the MacDonalds, MacLeods, MacLeans, and MacNeils. Until the Stewarts came to the throne of Scotland, the Outer Hebrides had been under the suzerainty of Norwegian Kings from the ninth century. Like their Nordic forebears, the clansmen of the Long Island are legendary seafarers and many Hebridean clan chiefs—including the MacNeils—proudly display on their coats of arms the black Lymphad or galley, echoing the infamous Viking longboat of their ancestors.

Barra is also one of the smallest of the permanently inhabited islands in the Western Hebrides. Solely occupied by the overproud MacNeils, they claim a traditional Celtic descent from the legendary Irish king of the fourth century, Niall of the Nine Hostages—whom is thus mythically esteemed as the "first" Chief of the MacNeils of Barra. However, DNA reveals that the MacNeils, in the direct male line, are actually of Norse extraction. Nevertheless, clan tradition relates that there was even a chief of the MacNeils at the time of the Biblical Great Flood—that particular MacNeil turned down an offer to board the Ark, saying he would not require Noah's assistance as he already had his own boat! From medieval times also comes the legend that once the laird himself had supped, his herald would mount the walls of Kisimul castle, blow a great horn from atop, and proclaim—to each point of the compass: "Hear, O ye people, and listen, O ye nations! The great MacNeil of Barra having finished his meal, the princes of the earth may dine!" (MacNeil, p. 62). In reality, their origins are obscure and the first documentary mention of a MacNeil of Barra is in a charter of 1427.

This overweening pride—and Viking blood—threw forth many remarkable leaders of the clan MacNeil, none more so than Ruadhri, or Roderick, MacNeil of Barra, chief during the reign of King James VI. Rory's eventful life spanned some sixty-three years between 1550 and 1613—a remarkable feat in such a turbulent age. Clan sennachies immortalized Roderick as the fifteenth laird of Barra and thirty-fifth Chief of the Name from Niall of the Nine Hostages; his Gaelic sobriquet was Ruadrhi an Taitear. Mistranslated as Rory the Tatar or Tartar, The Turbulent is closer in meaning. Nonetheless, comparing Rory The Tartar's deeds to the eponymous wild and barbaric Turkic tribes of the Central Asian steppes is indeed a fitting metaphor.

Rory The Turbulent MacNeil of Barra thrived in a violent era. The first historic mention of him is in 1598 when he joined a raid to the island of Islay, a MacDonald stronghold, alongside other Hebridean chiefs. At Bern Bige in Islay, "a sanguinary battle ensued with young [MacLean of] Duart and his allies victorious. They remained for three days killing all the MacDonalds, men, women, and children who could not escape, leaving Islay desolate" (MacNeil, p. 62). However, this bloody episode was but one of Rory The Tartar's many nefarious deeds.

Images by Shutterstock

Rory MacNeil of Barra's main claim to fame is his piratical career, notably for his success at harrying the shipping of Queen Elizabeth of England. Supporting the Tudor subjugation of Ireland, English merchant vessels and warships regularly crossed the Irish Sea to resupply their garrisons. That meant rich cargos sailing around the Antrim coastline just 120 nautical miles from Barra. The closeness and accessibility of this bounty was too much for Rory The Tatar to resist.

Rory's descendant would write some three hundred years later, "the Chief was particularly active in securing additional income by exploits of piracy, in which he was a past master, but like the pitcher and the well, went once too often..." (MacNeil, p.

62). The frequency and ferocity of Rory's depredations against English merchantmen soon reached the notice of Queen Elizabeth herself. Fed-up with these acts of lawlessness against her own subjects, the Queen admonished her cousin (and putative heir) King James VI to put an immediate stop to Rory's illicit exploits and bring the recalcitrant clan chief to justice. However, that was easier said than done, for "the King, knowing by past experience the difficulty, if not impossibility of securing a Hebridean Chief by force, decided to employ strategy..." (MacNeil, p. 63). In other words, King James would resort to subtle trickery to apprehend Rory The Turbulent.

The king thus tapped an equally turbulent and devious man with bringing Rory The Tartar to justice: Roderick MacKenzie, laird of Coigeach (1579-1626). Better known as the Tutor of Kintail, he was guardian to the underage chief of the MacKenzie clan. The king was well aware of MacKenzie's reputation for ruthlessness; the saying was: "There are only two things worse than the Tutor of Kintail, frost in spring and mist in the dog-days!" (MacKenzie, p. 408). One apocryphal story aptly illustrates the fierceness of Rory MacKenzie:

"On another occasion, when Sir Rorie was passing through Athole on his way to Edinburgh, he was stopped by the men of Athole for passing through their country without the leave of their lord. The Tutor of Kintail dismounted and sought out a stone, on which he began to sharpen his claymore. The Athole men, from a safe distance, asked him what he was doing there. 'I am going to make a road,' was the ready answer. 'You shall make no road here!' said the Athole men. 'Oh, I don't seek to do so; but I shall make it between your lord's head and his shoulders if I am hindered from pursuing my lawful business,' replied the Tutor. At this the Athole men retired, and, on reaching their lord, told him what had happened. 'It can only be two people, either the Devil or the

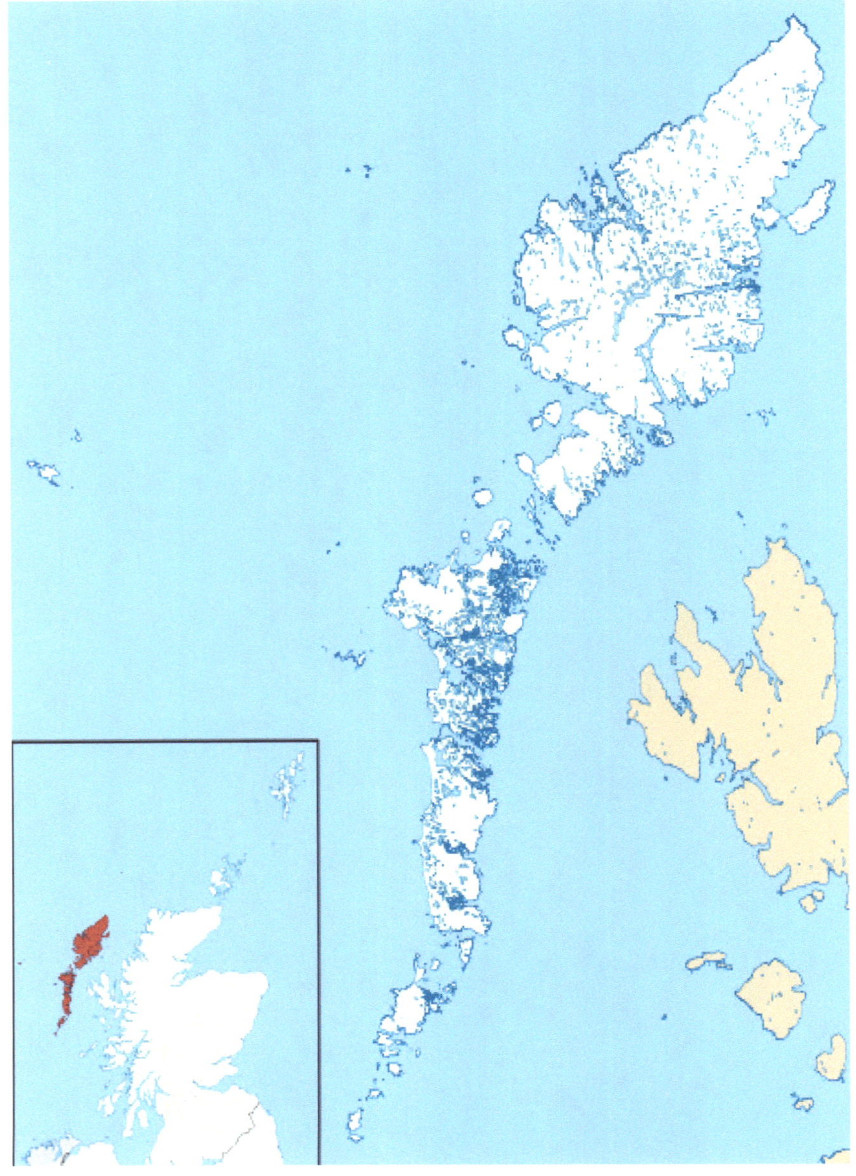

Images provided by Wikipedia Commons

Tutor of Kintail!' the lord said, 'let him have a free path by here forever.'" (MacKenzie, pp. 408-409.)

King James surely picked the right man for the task of bringing Rory The Turbulent to justice. The Tutor of Kintail knew Rory MacNeil was a shrewd man, safe and secure in his remote island fastness and castle of Kisimul, guarded by hundreds of loyal armed clansmen. MacKenzie therefore disguised himself as a humble merchant, innocently sailing into Castlebay on a sham trading voyage. The incognito Tutor then entered Kisimul Castle on the pretext of having luxury goods to sell to the covetous chief. MacKenzie explained to MacNeil that his ship encountered a French merchantman bound from Norway to Ireland—and thereby acquired some fine Bordeaux claret. The Tutor then graciously offered the pick of this cargo to MacNeil if only he would repair onboard to select them in-person. This was "an opportunity too rare to be lost, and Rory, full of anticipation, quickly accepted the invitation and boarded the ship. The mellow wines were soon in evidence; but alas! The crew had secured the hatches and weighed anchor!" A most disconcerted MacNeil

chief was now a prisoner, bound for the gallows of Edinburgh (MacNeil, p. 63).

But before being sent to his doom, Rory was granted an audience with King James VI himself. The king was "greatly surprised to see, instead of a weather beaten old ruffian, a kindly and courtly old gentleman in a long flowing beard" (MacNeil, p. 63). But the canny chief had a clever plan to charm his way out of danger; when asked by the king why he was preying on Elizabeth Tudor's merchants, Rory The Turbulent replied, "he [Rory] thought he was doing His Majesty a favor in harassing the subjects of the woman who had killed His Majesty's mother [i.e., Mary, Queen of Scots]!" (MacNeil, p. 64). King James could not deny the truth of MacNeil's clever assertion—but did not appreciate Rory's impertinence; the outraged king shouted, "The Devil take the carle! Rorie [MacKenzie], take him with you again, and dispose of him and his fortune as you please!" MacNeil astutely avoided the hangman but lost his lands as the Tutor of Kintail would henceforth be his feudal superior in Barra—presumedly to keep a close eye on the old pirate!

Despite this narrow escape, Rory The Tartar and his clan never really changed their ways. In January 1610 a French merchantman arrived in Castlebay seeking refuge after suffering storm damage. Rory's sons eagerly clambered onboard—uninvited—and proceeded to pillage the cargo, killing or wounding four or five crewmen. Rory The Turbulent was ordered apprehended for this latest depredation; although the MacNeil himself evaded capture, his sons were caught and sent in chains to Glasgow.

Queen Elizabeth I's reign is renowned for the exploits of her Sea Dogs, achieving fame and fortune preying upon Spanish vessels and colonies. Men like Drake and Raleigh were lionized by contemporary writers while Elizabeth largely ignored their brutal and barely legal methods. However, when English merchants were the victims of similar depredations, the outraged Queen did not hesitate to act. Focusing on one extraordinary man, Rory The Turbulent MacNeil of Barra, Elizabeth demanded that King James apprehend and punish the Scottish pirate—but Rory was far too canny for either sovereign and escaped due punishment by a most clever—and amusing—ruse!

The Old Trojan, Donald MacLeod, the Laird of Unish and Bernera, was the last of his kind. A chieftain and commander of his clan during the Jacobite Rebellions, he defied his own chief and brought his MacLeods "out" for the Stuarts in 1715 and 1745. A noble descendant of the mighty Norse founders of the Clan MacLeod, Domnhuill mac Iain mac Tormod i'c Leoid—Donald, son of John, son of Norman MacLeod—was a Scottish warrior and leader without peer. Cast in the mold of the medieval Viking warlords who conquered the islands of Scotland's Western Hebrides, Donald MacLeod earned the epithet of The Old Trojan on the battlefields of Sheriff Muir, Falkirk, and Culloden. In his long life of eighty-plus years, The Old Trojan married three times, had twenty-six children, played a role in the mysterious disappearance of Lady Grange, was involved with the Ship of the People episode, and fought in the Seaweed Wars. Through it all, The Old Trojan witnessed and resisted the decline of the traditional Scottish clan system as the rebellions strained then broke the ancient and traditional bonds between clansmen and clan chiefs. Largely set in the chaotic period between the Glorious Revolution of 1688 and the Battle of Culloden in 1746, this is a lively account of one of the last of the Scottish warlords who would forever disappear with the coming of the Highland Clearances. Readers interested in the historic Scottish clans of the Hebrides, especially the MacLeods, will find in this novel a gripping tale, based on real people and events, of those chaotic times.

D. G. MACDOUGALL

**BUY "THE OLD TROJAN"
AT AMAZON**

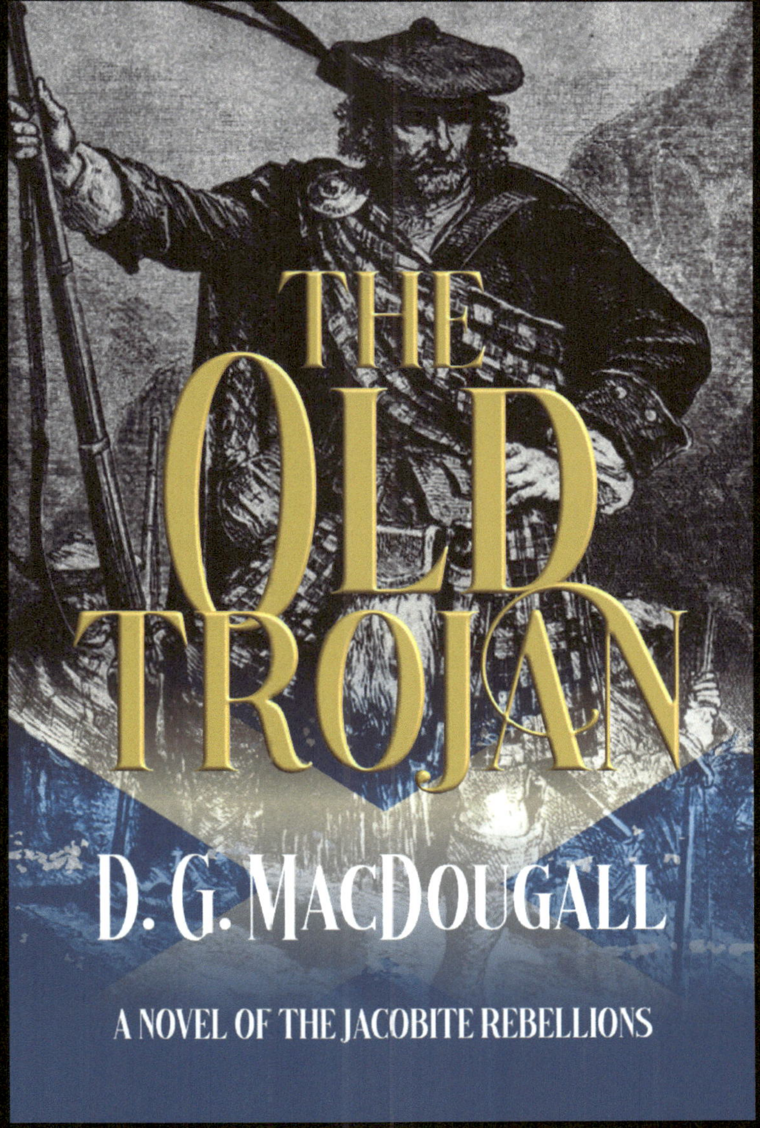

ISABELLA WHITNEY, SAGE POET TO YOUNG GENTLEWOMEN AND ALL OTHERS MAIDS IN LOVE

CONNIE BRIONES

When Elizabeth I ascended the throne in 1558, the Protestant reformers in England wanted her to reclaim Protestantism as the true faith of England, as it was during the reign of her brother, Edward VI (1547-1553). With the Protestant queen, Elizabeth, the reformers got their wish, and Protestantism regained its legitimacy as the true faith of England.

The Protestant Reformation ushered in changes to the way people worshipped. With its emphasis on individual salvation and the private reading of scriptures, learning to read in English became essential when English supplanted Latin as the primary language of religious literature and instruction. What was once the prerogative of males, females learned to read, albeit many just acquired rudimentary skills. For those few highly literate women in reading and writing with a knowledge of a foreign language, the Protestant reformers welcomed their help in propagating the church's teachings, achieving this principally through translations of religious texts.

While the Protestant Reformation gave women the gift of reading, its leaders couldn't predict the effect the booming printing industry of the mid-sixteenth century, with its vast array of books on a myriad of subjects available to a growing number of women readers, would have on literate women who had the desire to write. Isabella Whitney, an aspiring poet, was one of those women.

Despite the plethora of books that flooded the literary marketplace of London, women were meant to read books deemed suitable for preparing them for the only role they were destined to fulfill, that of wife and mother. Publishers catered to women with books on all sorts of topics on housewifery and childrearing. The increasing number of romance stories were off limits and mothers were expected to closely monitor what their daughters were reading. The sole purpose of a young woman's reading was to mold her into the ideal Protestant women of virtue, possessing traits of silence, obedience, modesty, and chastity.

Romance books posed more of a danger to the vulnerable young members of the female sex not yet occupied with tasks of housewifery and child-rearing. Juan Vives, Renaissance humanist and educational theorist of the early sixteenth century whose advice in *The Education of a Christian Woman*, remained the standard guide for rearing girls into young adulthood, wrote of romance books: Women will mistake false for true, harmful for salutary, foolish and senseless for serious and commendable. Women, believed to have inherited Eve's weak and gullible nature, would be titillated by romance stories, endangering the loss of their chastity. How then did it come to pass that in this controlled reading environment for women, Isabella Whitney, a young poet in her early twenties, wrote and published poetry about the taboo subject of man-women relations in love and challenged readers to determine which sex was more constant and true in love?

Isabella Whitney was an unusual, fully literate young woman from the middle ranks of society with superior skills in reading and writing. The publication of her first volume of poetry , The Copy of a Letter, lately written in meter, by a Young Gentlewoman: to her inconstant Lover with its adjoining poem, The Admonition of the Author to All Young Gentlewomen and All Other Maids Being in Love (1567) established her as the first English woman to write and publish secular poetry in the mid-sixteenth century.

Only scant biographical information exists about Isabella Whitney, forcing scholars to rely on her poetry which details major events in her life, to fill in the information gaps. We know for sure that she was born into a middle-class family in Cheshire, England, between 1546 and 1548 and most likely died after 1580. Like most young women of the middle class, she left home to work in domestic service to hone her housewifery skills for her future role as a wife and mother. Due to an unknown scandal, she was dismissed from her last domestic job as a live-in maidservant in London. Based on details from her poem, The Copy of a Letter, it's believed her dismissal was due to a failed love affair with a man who very likely worked in the same home and is, in fact, the inconstant Lover she addresses her poem to.

Rather than return home after losing her job, she decided to remain in London and make a living as a writer. In a verse epistle addressed to her sister, she writes Had I a husband, or a house, and all that belongs thereto — myself could frame about to rouse, as other women do: But till some household cares me tie, my books and pen I will apply. The poem, Will and Testament, which appears in her second volume of poetry, illustrates that her stay in London was made difficult by the unsavory conditions of city life incurred by living on a shoestring budget.

A pivotal literary event occurred in 1566 that rendered the publishing opportunity Isabella Whitney longed for. The English translation of Heroides by the Roman poet Ovid hit London's book market and was favorably received by the urban reading public. Ovid's translated work mirrored a theme popular with London's growing middle-class readers - what is a woman's true nature? Many authors attempted to answer it and gave readers contrasting answers. Most printed material portrayed women in the negative. Among the most popular descriptors for women were vain, querulous, gossiping, deceitful, manipulative, conniving, and immoral. And a few rallied to defend women who argued they possessed exemplary qualities. This long-standing tradition of questioning a woman's true nature began in France in the early fifteenth century and was known as the Querelle des Femme; the English dubbed it the woman question. The gendered sparring became popular with men and women as they traded barbs and jibes based on their reading.

What made Ovid's Heroides distinct was his use of verse epistles and expressing in a woman's voice the grievances of fifteen heroines of Greek and Roman mythology, wherein they addressed the heroic lovers who mistreated or abandoned them. The new format was coined The Heroidean complaint form, and the reading public of London, many comprised of men and women from the middle ranks of society, clamored for more. Always with his finger on the pulse of his readership, London printer and bookseller Richard Jones looked to the poems of Isabella Whitney to give them what they wanted.

Richard Jones was known for his publications of popular literature, mainly ballads, poetry, plays, and prose romance. He offered Isabella the opportunity to write in the new Heroidean complaint form. She was ready for it, having been well read in Ovid's work, not just Heroides but also his Art of Love, and that of another Roman poet, Virgil's epic poem, The Aeneid. She organized and constructed the stanzas of her poems with selected tales of heroines from these translated works, aligning them with her message that men were not to be trusted in love. Like the heroines in Ovid's Heroides, she addresses her grievances against the man who jilted her in The Copy of a Letter. In her adjoining poem, she speaks to the young women of London seeking love and warns them to beware of men's falseness.

As a marketing tool, Richard Jones decided to include two poems by men in the same pamphlet with Isabella's poems, A Love Letter, or an Earnest Persuasion of a Lover, in which the author complains about the woman who broke their betrothal without explanation, and A Warning to All Young Men to Beware the Feigned Fidelity of Inconstant Maidens. The subjects and themes of the two poems written by men bear a striking similarity to Isabella's poetry, The Copy of a Letter… to an Unfaithful Lover and An Admonition by the Author to all young Gentlewomen: And to all other Maids in Love. A small anthology of poetry counterpointing female and male complaints about women-men relationships in love emerged from the union of these poems, a common feature of the Querelle des Femme tradition but written in the Heroidean complaint form.

What made Isabella's first volume of poetry significant was that it challenged the prevailing view of conservative educational theorists and prominent Protestant reformers who asserted that women were incapable of rational thought and, therefore, couldn't make sense of the text they read without guidance. Not only did Isabella prove that women could do more than recall the words of what they read, but they could interpret, analyze, and evaluate, arriving at their own logical conclusions without assistance. She builds her stanzas with carefully selected references to the tales of the classical Roman and Greek myths she read. And after contemplation, she concludes that the actions of the Greek and Roman heroes so long lauded by men are underserved. Discerning their false wooing and ultimate betrayals, she doesn't hesitate to state her opinion: For they, for their unfaithfulness, did get perpetual fame: Fame? Wherefore did I term it so? I should have called it shame.

Referencing characters from the classical love stories in her poems, Isabella reveals that she has read these forbidden stories for women. And yet, she has not been led astray from the path of virtue as men feared, thereby casting doubt on the common percept that if women are allowed to read romance stories, they will inevitably exchange their virtuous way of life for a lascivious one. She doesn't praise the crazed actions of the abandoned women: Medea's vengeful killing of her children over Jason's betrayal, or Dido, who was so distraught when her lover, Aeneas, left her; she killed herself. Nor is there approval of women surrendering their good sense to passion once they are smitten with a man. She upholds the character of Hero, the virgin priestess of the Greek God of Love, Aphrodite, as the model to emulate as seen in her relationship with Leander: Hero did try Leander's truth, before that she did trust: therefore she found him unto her both constant true and just. But like Leander there be few, therefore in time take heed: And always try before you trust , so shall you better speed. Isabella's calm tone urges women to practice restraint in the beginning stage of courtship. Such advice reflects prudence and temperance, traits associated with women of virtue. No man could assert Isabella's head was turned away from virtuous behavior for having read tales of romance.

Isabella continued her association with Richard Jones, who published and sold her second volume of poetry, A Sweet Nosegay (1573). Although she dreamed of being a working writer, she still had to support herself working as a domestic. But Isabella Whitney accomplished what no other English woman did before her, to write secular poetry at a time when women were meant to be seen and not heard. And with her first volume of poetry, which is the focus of this article, she aimed to make all readers, men, and women, aware of the inaccurate portrayal of her sex in print. From a modern viewpoint, it is easy to see the early stirrings of feminism.

Familiar and friendly Epistles,
I neuer yet to rue my smart,
did finde that thou hadst pitie:
wherefore small cause ther is, & I
should greeue from thee go:
But many women foolyshly,
lyke me, and other moe:
Doe such a fyred fancy set,
on those which least deserue,
That long it is ere wit we get,
away from them to swarue.
But tyme with pittie ott wyl tel
to those that wil her try:
whether it best be moze to mell,
or vtterly defye.
And now hath time me put i mind,
of thy great cruelnes:
That neuer once a help wold finde,
to ease me in distres.
Thou neuer yet, woldst credit geue

before her departyng.
Yet am I in no angry moode,
but wyll, or ere I goe
In perfect loue and charytie.
my Testament here write:
And leaue to thee such Treasurye,
as I in it recyte.
Now stand a side and geue me leaue
to write my latest Wyll:
And see that none you do deceaue,
of that I leaue them tyl.

The maner of her

Wyll, & what she left to London:
and to all those in it: at her departing.

I Whole in body, and in minde,
but very weake in Purse:
Do make, and write my Testament
for feare it wyll be wurse.
And fyrst I wholy do commend,
my Soule and Body eke:
To God the Father and the Son,
so long as I can speake.
And after speach: my Soule to hym,
and Body to the Graue;
Tyll time that all shall rise agayne,
Iudgement for to haue.   And

B.iii.

T.B. in prayse of the Autor.
And that it is no fable, you shall see:
For here at large the sequell will declare
To Cuntrey warde, her loue and friendly care.

* The smelling Flowers of an Arbor sweete,
An Orcharde pickt, presented is to thee:
And for her seconde worke, she thought it meete,
sithe Maides with loftie stile may not agree:
In hoape hereby, somthynge to pleasure thee,
And when her busie care from head shall lurke,
She practize will, and promise longer worke.

* Now happie Dames, if good deserueth well,
her praise for Flowers philosophicall:
And let your Branches twyned that excell
her head adorne: wherin she floorish shall:
And BERRIE so, resies alwaies at your call,
The purple blew, the red, the white I baue,
To wrappe amyd your Garlands fresh & braue.

FINIS.   THO. BIR.

¶ A sweete

A sweet Nosgay,

Or pleasant Posye: contayning a
hundred and ten Phylosophicall
Flowers. &c.

¶ The I. Flower.
SVch freendes as haue ben absent
moze ioyful be at meeting (long
Then those which euer presēt are
and dayly haue their greetyng.

¶ The II
When peryls they are present, then
doth absence keepe thee free:
Whereas, if that thou present werte
might dangers light on thee.

The III.
The presence of the mynd must be
preferd, if we do well:
Aboue the bodyes presence; for
it farre doth it excell.
B.ii.

The

CONNIE BRIONES

Connie Briones has a Masters in Women's History which informs her writing. She first learned of Isabella Whitney while writing her thesis on
The Development of Women's Literary
in Tudor England.

She is working on a historical novel about the young adult life of Isabella Whitney.

COMING SOON!

THE ALLURE

OF KIT MARLOWE

D. K. MARLEY

Imagine this: meandering down a corridor in the great Globe Theatre full of relics of the past, all speaking William Shakespeare's name. But, of course, before that day you had no reason to consider any other name nor had any such thought been presented to you. And then, it happens. You round the corner and before you is a wall that displays the names and faces of five men that could have been the writer of the plays.

This is what happened to me. I perused the names with interest and amazement. Like finding a rare antique at a yard sale that someone missed, Christopher Marlowe's face stared back at me and my heart skipped a beat. How could the world have missed the obvious; how could I? The sparkling little trinket of truth that spoke to me as if his ghost whispered in my ear, "Tell my story. Foul deeds will rise though all the world o'erwhelm them to men's eyes."

I suppose I could have chosen any of the men, but something moved me. From the very moment, Marlowe's allure buried in his mysterious eyes made me know a story lay there hidden, waiting to burst forth. Within a week and endless hours on the internet and at the library, the clues he left behind, the secret little smile in his Cambridge portrait and the knowing glint in his eyes lay before me. The pieces of the puzzle fit together like never before: the treasured words of Christopher Marlowe, the Muse's Darling, and not the man from Stratford, linked into a beautiful and tragic telling of a man who knew the world. Here was the man who travelled the continent, who knew court life and country travails, politics and provocateurs, religion, science, languages, intrigue, love, betrayal, and exile. All the meaty experience to fill the pages of mighty plays and sonnets.

One of the first things that we are told as writers is, "Write what you know." The adage cannot have changed since the 16th century. Marlowe wrote what he knew, leaving behind the clues, which were a common and clever tool used by writers of the day. So I ask, why buy a reproduction when you can have the real thing? It's a lot more fun to dig for authentic Marlovian gold than float along with the crowd picking up synthetic Shakespearean souvenirs.

And if you listen closely, you may hear his voice, as well. "I have a whole school of tongues in this belly of mine, and not a tongue of them all speaks any other word but my name."

SIMPLICITY VERSUS ACADEMIA

Galileo said, "Facts which at first seem improbable will, even on scant explanation, drop the cloak which has hidden them and stand forth in naked and simple beauty."

Simplicity often reveals truth, whereas there is confusion in an overabundance of words. I do not claim to be an academic, nor do I ascribe to the level of a scholar who spends her days wrangling with Stratfordians about the identity of "Mr. W.H." or "the Dark Lady." I am simply a writer who finds beauty in words, the way certain phrases roll off the tongue, the transcending feeling that a mere paragraph can invoke, or when a novel shows the commonality of the human condition. In that beauty, that naked and simple beauty, stands stark truth uncluttered by a convocation of words. At last, seeing the forest and not just the trees.

Facts that Stratfordians voice as improbable - the fact that Christopher Marlowe is the true writer of the plays and sonnets - even on scant explanation, such as I am able to produce being as I am just another common enthusiast, has indeed, to my mind, dropped the cloak which has hidden them and stands bared for all the world to see. Truth is simple. Truth is the one person shouting that the emperor is naked when all others shut their eyes, look away or refuse to believe. And the simplicity of it relates to the everyday ordinary person, which is the vast majority of the world.

If the world was able to be presented with the simple facts concerning Christopher Marlowe, as I was, there would be no more doubting. Even if the academic world can never produce solid evidence, we have more than reasonable doubt here that William Shakespeare had the skills, education, knowledge of languages, etc. to produce such profound verse. Simply put, he was an actor, not a playwright or poet. Christopher "Kit" Marlowe, on the other hand, was gifted at an early age with skills that exceeded his years. Educated at the best schools and sur-

rounded by those who prodded him, he travelled to the continent, he excelled in languages and proved himself a capable playwright and poet well before his twentieth year. Where was Shakespeare during those years? Still in Stratford, married with three children, with no evidence that he wrote a single thing.

Again, Galileo, an academic himself, revealed the answer in relation to these two men. Simple truth trumps pretentious fabrications any day. All you have to do is to remove the veil from your eyes, to stop gorging on the Shakespearean propaganda fed to you through the years, and hear the ring of truth sounded in Marlowe's own words in Sonnet 76: "Why write I still all one, ever the same, and keep invention in a noted weed, that every word doth almost tell my name, showing their birth and where they did proceed?"

*****

Articles previously published at www.marlowe-shakespeare.blogspot.com - The Shakespeare-Marlowe Connection

*****

In 2007, I had the rare privilege of attending the Authorship debate at the Globe Theatre in London, a small gathering hosted by Sir Derek Jacobi and Mark Rylance as they presented their preferred candidates as the man who wrote the plays. Sir Jacobi leaned towards the Edward de Vere, the Earl of Oxford, and Mr. Rylance pushed for his favourite, Francis Bacon. Of course, no one brought up Marlowe... that is, until the break where I approached Sir Jacobi and asked, "What about Marlowe?"

His first reaction was, "What is an American's interest in Marlowe or in the Authorship debate?" I told him a bit about my research for writing my book "Blood and Ink" and he wished me much success on my endeavours. While the rest of the debate remained on Bacon and Oxford, I must say I learned a great deal from these two illustrious Shakespearean actors. It is an experience I've remembered fondly through the years.

D. K. Marley

Images by Wikipedia

If you loved Ken Follett's "A Column of Fire," take another journey into 17th-century England with the 5-star reviewed alternate historical fiction novel, "Blood and Ink."

History shows Kit Marlowe died in a tavern brawl in Deptford in 1593, but did he? England is torn apart by religious metamorphosis and espionage. The stages of England and bright intellectual boys are used to bolster Queen Elizabeth I's reign and propagate the rising Protestant faith. At the age of eight, Christopher Marlowe, the muse's darling, is sucked into the labyrinth of secret spy rings, blood, murder, and betrayal, while his own ambition to become England's favorite playwright drifts further from his grasp.

As Christopher grows to manhood, he sinks further into the darkness, and a chance meeting with an unknown actor from Stratford-upon-Avon, William Shakespeare, sets him on a path of destiny - a fate of forced exile and the revelation that the real enemy is not an assassin of Rome, but a man who stared into his eyes and smiled. One he did not expect...

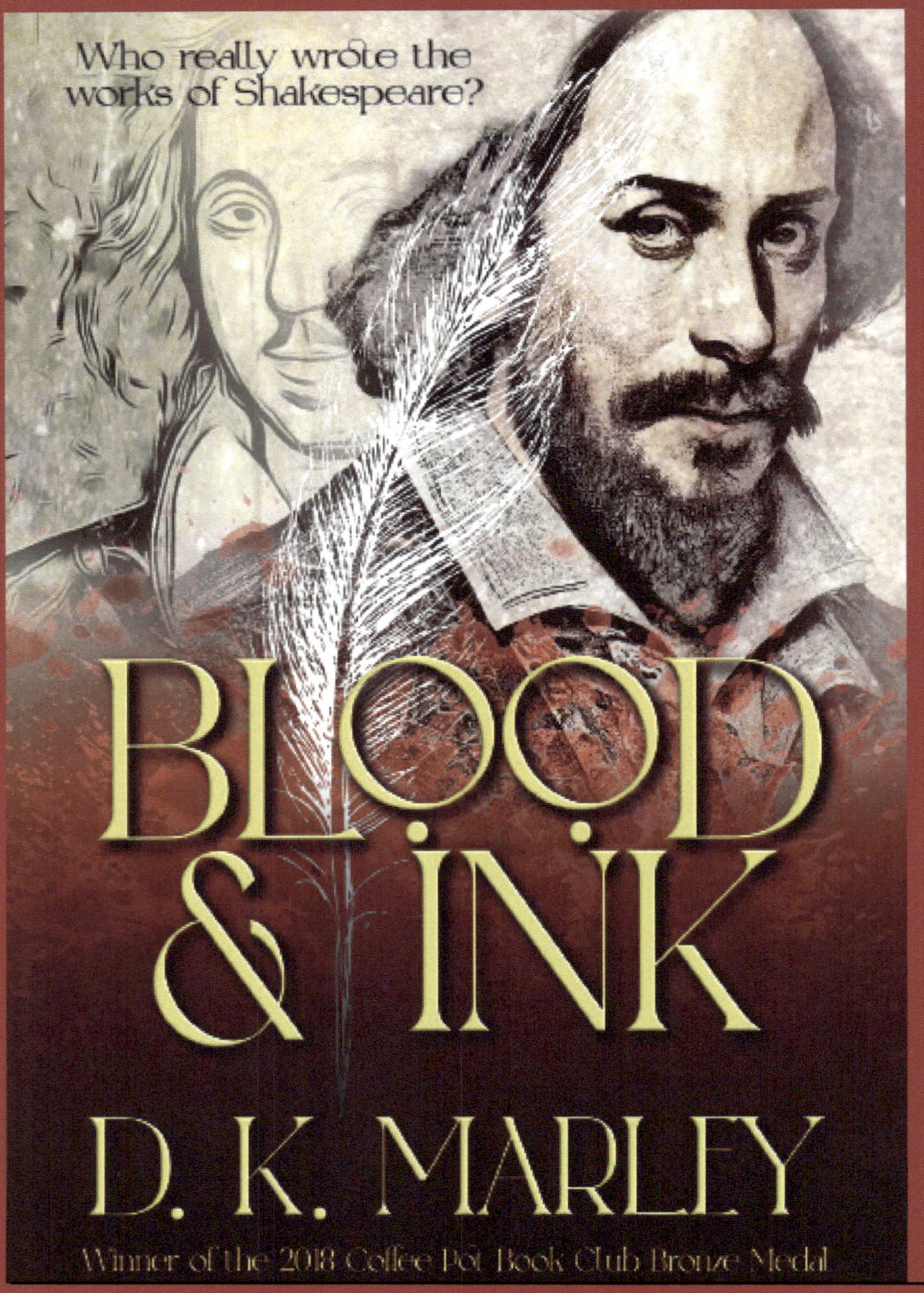

D. K. Marley is a historical fiction author specializing in Shakespearean-themed books, as well as her new time-travel series which spans the centuries from WWI to the days of King Arthur.

Her Shakespeare-based book:

"Blood and Ink"
"The Fire of Winter: a Lady Macbeth Novel"
"The Prince of Denmark"
"Star-Crossed"

Her time-travel novels:

"Kingfisher"
"Antipodes" - coming 2024

Her breakaway Southern novel:

"Child of Love & Water"

*****

AVAILABLE ON AMAZON

Visit D. K.'s Facebook page at facebook.com/therealdkmarley.author

A thrillingly provocative investigation into the Shakespeare authorship question, exploring how doubting that William Shakespeare wrote his plays became an act of blasphemy…and who the Bard might really be.

The theory that Shakespeare may not have written the works that bear his name is the most horrible, vexed, unspeakable subject in the history of English literature. Scholars admit that the Bard's biography is a "black hole," yet to publicly question the identity of the god of English literature is unacceptable, even (some say) "immoral."

In Shakespeare Was a Woman and Other Heresies, journalist and literary critic Elizabeth Winkler sets out to probe the origins of this literary taboo. Whisking readers from London to Stratford-upon-Avon to Washington, DC, she pulls back the curtain to show how the forces of nationalism and empire, religion and mythmaking, gender and class have shaped our admiration for Shakespeare across the centuries. As she considers the writers and thinkers—from Walt Whitman to Sigmund Freud to Supreme Court justices—who have grappled with the riddle of the plays' origins, she explores who may perhaps have been hiding behind his name. A forgotten woman? A disgraced aristocrat? A government spy? Hovering over the mystery are Shakespeare's plays themselves, with their love for mistaken identities, disguises, and things never quite being what they seem.

they seem.

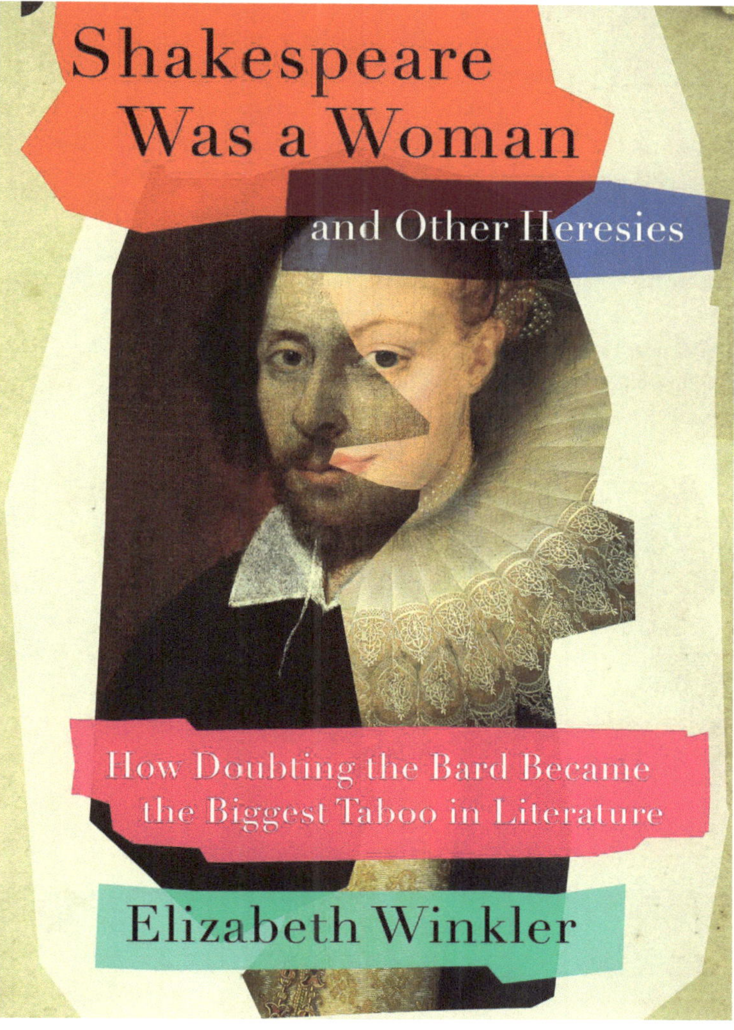

**AVAILABLE AT AMAZON or
SIMON & SCHUSTER**

RELEASED MAY 9, 2023 / SIMON & SCHUSTER

As she interviews scholars and skeptics, Winkler's interest turns to the larger problem of historical truth—and of how human imperfections (bias, blindness, subjectivity) shape our construction of the past. History is a story, and the story we find may depend on the story we're looking for.

An irresistible work of literary detection, Shakespeare Was a Woman and Other Heresies will forever change how you think of Shakespeare… and of how we as a society decide what's up for debate and what's just nonsense, just heresy.

EXCERPT:

Prologue

In England in the summer of 1964, an unusual case came before the courts. It involved a squabble over the will of Miss Evelyn May Hopkins and the authorship of the works of William Shakespeare. Miss Hopkins had died, leaving a third of her inheritance to the Francis Bacon Society for the purpose of finding the original manuscripts of Shakespeare's plays. She referred to them as the "Bacon-Shakespeare manuscripts," believing the true author of the works to have been Francis Bacon, the Elizabethan philosopher and statesman. The aim of finding the manuscripts was to prove that

Bacon was, in fact, the author of the works attributed to Shakespeare. Her heirs were not pleased. Naturally, they preferred that the money go to themselves. Seeking to reclaim their inheritance, the heirs brought a suit against the society, arguing that Miss Hopkins's provision should be set aside on the grounds that the search would be a "wild goose chase." To support their case, they solicited the testimony of scholarly experts. The Right Honorable Richard Wilberforce, a justice of Her Majesty's High Court, presided.

Counsel for the next of kin "described it as a wild goose chase; but wild geese can, with good fortune, be apprehended," observed the justice. Many discoveries are unlikely until they are made, he pointed out: "one may think of the Codex Sinaiticus, or the Tomb of Tutankhamen, or the Dead Sea Scrolls." Wilberforce was a stolid Englishman, a former classics scholar at Oxford University who rose through Britain's legal ranks to become a senior Law Lord in the House of Lords and a member of the Queen's Privy Council. Having reviewed the evidence submitted to the court, he summarized it as follows:

"The orthodox opinion, which at the present time is unanimous, or nearly so, among scholars and experts in sixteenth and seventeenth century literature and history, is that the plays were written by William Shakespeare of Stratford-upon-Avon, actor." However, Justice Wilberforce continued, "The evidence in favour of Shakespeare's authorship is quantitatively slight. It rests positively, in the main, on the explicit statements in the First Folio of 1623, and on continuous tradition; negatively on the lack of any challenge to this ascription at the time" of the First Folio's publication. Furthermore, the justice found, "There are a number of difficulties in the way of the traditional ascription… a number of known facts which are difficult to reconcile…. [S]o far from these difficulties tending to diminish with time, the intensive search of the nineteenth century has widened the evidentiary gulf between William Shakespeare the man, and the author of the plays."

The justice went on to consider the testimony of the scholarly experts. Kenneth Muir, King Alfred Professor of English literature at the University of Liverpool, supported the plaintiffs, Miss Hopkins's aggrieved heirs. He considered it "certain" that Bacon could not have written the works of Shakespeare. Hugh Trevor-Roper, Regius Professor of Modern History at the University of Oxford, departed slightly from his English literature colleagues, taking what the justice deemed "a more cautious line." Though Professor Trevor-Roper "definitely does not believe that the works of 'Shakespeare' could have been written by Francis Bacon, he also considers that the case for Shakespeare rests on a narrow balance of evidence and that new material could upset it; that though almost all professional scholars accept 'Shakespeare's' authorship, a settled scholarly tradition can inhibit free thought, that heretics are not necessarily wrong. His conclusion is that the question of authorship cannot be considered as closed."

Justice Wilberforce agreed. The question was not closed. The evidence for Shakespeare was too slim, the problems too many. The scholars might be wrong. Even if Francis Bacon was unlikely, new material might show someone other than Shakespeare to have been the author. Whoever wrote them, the manuscripts of Shakespeare's plays had never been found. Their discovery would be "of the highest value to history and to literature," Wilberforce proclaimed. Indeed, he added, to the consternation of the plaintiffs and the Shakespeare scholars, "the revelation of a manuscript would contribute, probably decisively, to a solution to the authorship problem, and this alone is benefit enough."

Miss Hopkins's bequest to the Francis Bacon Society was upheld.

Image Credit to Caroline Winkler

REVIEWS

"An extraordinarily brilliant and scholarly work, written with an unyielding sleuthing instinct and sparkling with pleasurably naughty moments. This page-turner is mesmerizing."
—André Aciman, PhD, New York Times bestselling author of Call Me by Your Name

"Elizabeth Winkler is blessed with the clear-eyed wit of a heroine in a Shakespearean comedy. Her undoing of the fools in the forest of the authorship question is iconoclasm As You Like It—joy to behold, lesson for us all."
—Lewis Lapham, founder of Lapham's Quarterly

"Lively…. Winkler is a crackerjack researcher, deftly laying out the myriad questions, arguments and mysteries swirling around Shakespeare."
—Michael Dirda, The Washington Post

"Elizabeth Winkler's Shakespeare Was a Woman and Other Heresies is one of the most engaging, riveting, scholarly, and challenging whodunits anyone with an interest in theater, human psychology, literature, and history can hope to read. Following in the footsteps of Henry James, Mark Twain, Mark Rylance, and innumerable other skeptics, Winkler writes about what has been essentially a centuries old theological dispute about the origins of Shakespeare's astounding body of work like a Shakespearean drama itself: full of complex characters with false reputations and deceptive appearances."
—Bessel van der Kolk, MD, New York Times bestselling author of The Body Keeps Score

"Winkler's prose is smooth, her jokes land, her synthesis

ELIZABETH WINKLER

Elizabeth Winkler is a journalist and book critic whose work has appeared in The Wall Street Journal, The New Yorker, The New Republic, The Times Literary Supplement, and The Economist, among other publications. She received her undergraduate degree from Princeton University and her master's in English literature from Stanford University. Her essay "Was Shakespeare a Woman?", first published in The Atlantic, was selected for The Best American Essays 2020. She lives in Washington, DC.

of the considerable amounts of research she's done is gracefully rendered, and she has a keen eye for the foibles of Shakespeare biographers."
—Slate

"No, Elizabeth Winkler doesn't reveal the true identity of the writer Ruth Bader Ginsburg termed "the literary genius known by the name William Shakespeare." But she does explain how we've wound up with, among an army of others, a republican Shakespeare and a monarchist Shakespeare, a Shakespeare who hated his wife and one who loved his, a Shakespeare who wrote all the plays and a Shakespeare who could not write at all. Along her intrepid way, Winkler charts, with refreshing clarity, the much-contested ground underfoot, studded with flinty convictions, gnarled fictions, and a surprising number of land mines."
—Stacy Schiff, Pulitzer Prize-winning author of The Revolutionary

"A perfect introduction to a world of unbridled passion, retribution, and intrigue—I refer of course to the Shakespeare authorship question. Brilliant and mind-blowing."
—Karen Joy Fowler, New York Times bestselling author of Booth

"A fascinating read. Winkler boldly pushes against traditional boundaries of gender and identity to show that meaning can be constructed in many different ways."
—Amanda Foreman, PhD, internationally bestselling author of Georgiana

"Deeply researched and fearlessly reported, this book takes on what Winkler terms the 'literary malpractice' and mob mentality of elite Shakespeare scholars invested in maintaining comfortable yet deeply problematic narratives. Shakespeare Was a Woman and Other Heresies is, at heart, an impassioned call to re-examine history and evidence (and lack thereof)—and to pursue scholarly truth even in the face of vicious opposition."
—Lesley Blume, New York Times bestselling author of Everybody Behaves Badly

"Delightful! Shakespeare Was a Woman and Other Heresies charms from beginning to end."
—Anonymous, author of Becoming Duchess Goldblatt

Named One of Esquire's 50 Best Biographies of All Time

The Pulitzer Prize and National Book Award finalist, reissued with a new afterword for the 400th anniversary of Shakespeare's death.

A young man from a small provincial town moves to London in the late 1580s and, in a remarkably short time, becomes the greatest playwright not of his age alone but of all time. How is an achievement of this magnitude to be explained? Stephen Greenblatt brings us down to earth to see, hear, and feel how an acutely sensitive and talented boy, surrounded by the rich tapestry of Elizabethan life, could have become the world's greatest playwright.

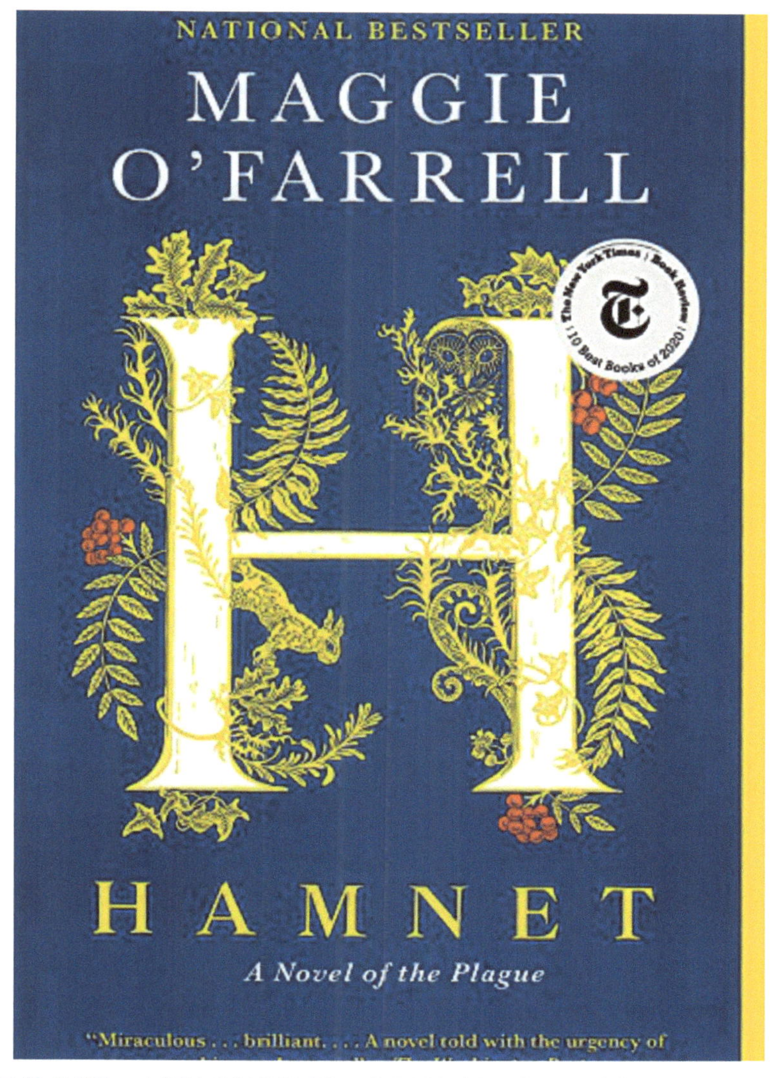

NATIONAL BOOK CRITICS CIRCLE AWARD WINNER • NEW YORK TIMES BESTSELLER • "Of all the stories that argue and speculate about Shakespeare's life ... here is a novel ... so gorgeously written that it transports you." —The Boston Globe

In 1580's England, during the Black Plague a young Latin tutor falls in love with an extraordinary, eccentric young woman in this "exceptional historical novel" (The New Yorker) and best-selling winner of the Women's Prize for Fiction.

Agnes is a wild creature who walks her family's land with a falcon on her glove and is known throughout the countryside for her unusual gifts as a healer, understanding plants and potions better than she does people. Once she settles with her husband on Henley Street in Stratford-upon-Avon she becomes a fiercely protective mother and a steadfast, centrifugal force in the life of her young husband, whose career on the London stage is taking off when his beloved young son succumbs to sudden fever.

A luminous portrait of a marriage, a shattering evocation of a family ravaged by grief and loss, and a tender and unforgettable re-imagining of a boy whose life has been all but forgotten, and whose name was given to one of the most celebrated plays of all time, Hamnet is mesmerizing, seductive, impossible to put down—a magnificent leap forward from one of our most gifted novelists.

'Not the fashion': Imagining the Formative Presence of Early Modern Women in Shakespeare's Circle

NAOMI MILLER

At the conclusion to *As You Like It,* Rosalind observes famously that 'It is not the fashion to see the lady the Epilogue' (Epilogue, 1-2). With more lines than any other female character in Shakespeare's plays, Rosalind's shrewd caution about what is 'not the fashion' for women's voices was at once seemingly contradicted and actually reinforced by the delivery of these lines by a boy actor playing a girl on Shakespeare's stage – signalling a matter of what an audience 'likes' to see. When considering biofictions about Shakespeare and early modern women, Rosalind's caution can be applied outside the frame of a single speech to acknowledge a gap between appearance and reality, aspiration and consequence.

Contemporary biofictions about Shakespeare have entertained multiple possibilities for early modern women who might have influenced the playwright in his female characterizations, fulfilling what one might take to be the modern authors' implicit aspirations to celebrate little-known women's voices. And yet the majority of these women are represented in the roles of lover and/or muse, often with little regard for the women's own voices and roles in the historical record. Playwrights and novelists have found irresistible the temptation to put a name to Shakespeare's 'Dark Lady', perpetuating a modern 'fashion' for casting various historical or fictional women in that role, while emphasizing their importance primarily in the passive positions of inspiration or influence. In contrast, in this chapter I consider biofictional representations of Mary Sidney Herbert, Aemilia Lanyer, and Mary Wroth on both page and stage, and explore the differential consequences of the fashion for claiming women's fictionalized influence over Shakespeare, by attending to their own historical voices.

Playing with multiple possibilities associated with the Shakespeare authorship debate, actor and theatre director Mark Rylance's play *I Am Shakespeare* entertains a range of candidates for the position, including 'Mary Sidney Herbert, the Countess of Pembroke, to whose sons the First Folio was dedicated' (2012: 68). Rylance's very modern Countess links her relationship with her 'hidden lover, Dr Lister,' to the 'forbidden relations across class boundaries [in] so many of the love affairs in Shakespeare works' (Ibid., 71). The Countess's formative role as an influence upon Shakespeare becomes visible in the reference to her adaptive translation of Garnier's tragedy *Marc Antoine* (the first play about Antony and Cleopatra in English blank verse), in which she claims that she 'used the idea of translated historical drama as a veiling device to tell the truth' (Ibid., 73). And indeed, Rylance uses his own play as a veiling device to suggest, in her voice, that 'it would certainly be refreshing to hear the opinions of some other women' (Ibid., 84), particularly where Shakespeare is concerned. Rylance gives credit to Robin Williams's argument in *Sweet Swan of Avon* that Mary Sidney Herbert was the author of Shakespeare's plays in convincing him that 'the brilliant Mary Sidney [...] may throw important light on the mysterious authorship of the Shakespeare plays and poems' (Williams 2012: back cover). Yet he takes a detour in making the creative choice, as playwright, to represent the Countess of Pembroke in a surprise reveal as not a Sidney after all, but the love-child of Queen Elizabeth, and as the lover rather than sister of Philip Sidney. So despite his inclusion of the Countess in his theatrical roster of Shakespeare authorship candidates, Rylance nonetheless replicates the pattern of representing a woman author as the lover of a more famous man.

Before the publication of my own novel, *Imperfect Alchemist* (2020), Mary Sidney Herbert had not yet received extensive treatment in biofictions, whether on the page or the stage. She does have a walk-on role in the second novel of Deborah Harkness's All Souls trilogy, *Shadow of Night* (2012), where she's introduced to the reader as 'the foremost woman of letters in the country, and Sir Philip Sidney's sister' (223). However the Countess of Pembroke's role in this novel, and in series 2 of the television series spinoff (*A Discovery of Witches* (2021)), is not that of the eloquent author of her own play and poems, but a figure connected to magic. At her first meeting with Diana Bishop, for instance, an embroidered bee and snake magically detach themselves from Mary Sidney's slippers and escape of their own accord. Along those lines, the television series represents her onscreen as a woman whose alchemical expertise connects her to other magical figures in that fantasy world, rather than to other authors, whether male or female.

I was encouraged by a trade editor to pitch my novel about Mary Sidney Herbert, *Imperfect Alchemist*, by referencing Harkness's novels and the television series because the Countess had popular 'name recognition' through that series that might appeal to publishers. However, because I was interested in featuring the Countess in my own biofiction as a female scientist and published author who mentored other women authors, rather than as a magician, I composed my novel with primary reference to Mary Sidney Herbert's own voice – in her *Psalms,* her play *Antonius,* and her completion of Philip Sidney's *Arcadia.*

In *Imperfect Alchemist,* Shakespeare is moved and inspired by reading Mary Sidney Herbert's play, *Antonius*, and by meeting her when he brings his players to perform *As You Like It* at Wilton House, where he accepts a commission from her to produce a play about Antony and Cleopatra for the public stage. The following passage illustrates Shakespeare's point of view:

> Antonius had infused his consciousness from its opening speech, a paean to a goddess in the voice of a general willing to risk all for love. While her adept verse drew him in from the start, it is her characterization of the indomitable Queen that still holds him in thrall. A Cleopatra of head-turning complexity – lover and mother, seeker and ruler, coward and hero, flawed and yet complete. He has mulled over the tragedy and wrestled with its contradictions ever since, tempted to take on the story himself.
>
> No such character has ever appeared on the English stage. Nor is likely to, he understands, unless he writes her himself, for the Countess's convention-breaking Antonius was composed not for the public stage but for a courtly circle more primed for paradox than the larger public, who tend to like their villains dark and their heroes dazzling. What a challenge rendering a Cleopatra inspired by Antonius would be – to show the public a female monarch who rules both an empire and a Roman general's heart, with a touch as deft as it is ruthless – and to make the audience fall in love with her for the invincible willfulness that is her greatest strength and vulnerability in one.
>
> Even as her play captured his attention, so must his own transmutation of the story capture hers. He's convinced that any celebration of this queen's infinite variety must commence with dark before light, shadows before bright possibility. It remains to be seen how she will treat a playwright who aspires not to contradict his patron's vision, but to complicate it. This Countess makes hungry where most she satisfies.
>
> (Miller 2020: 331-32)

Subsequently, the Countess collaborates with Shakespeare on the play that becomes his *Antony and Cleopatra*. These passages include excerpts from her *Antonius* as well as Shakespeare's play. An accomplished alchemist as well as author, she inspires Shakespeare to envision both their collaborative partnership and the relationship between Antony and Cleopatra in terms of the hermaphroditic ideal of alchemy, which brings together spirit and matter, male and female, Sol and Luna.

Constructing a biofictional frame that extends far beyond Mary Sidney Herbert's authorial collaboration with Shakespeare, I include the voices of other women authors in my narrative. As I explain in the author's note: 'Responding to her known patronage of women authors such as Aemilia Lanyer and her goddaughter, Mary Wroth, I have imagined some of these women into the Countess's writers' circle, their interaction with the male authors inspiring visions of new possibilities', while 'my account of Mary's collaboration with Shakespeare is another fiction that is not beyond the realm of possibility' (Miller 2020: 440). Again, placing women authors centre stage, I include an imagined performance of *Antonius* at Wilton House, where Mary Wroth plays Cleopatra and Aemilia Lanyer plays Charmian. At the close of their collaboration, Shakespeare tells the Countess, 'Together we have crafted a play unlike any I have written before – a play of communion across boundaries'. Which also, Mary reflects, 'expanded the boundaries of her own vision while connecting with his. A worthwhile experiment' (Miller 2020: 361). Unlike Mark Rylance, I'm concerned to bring Mary Sidney Herbert's published words, as a dramatist in particular, to modern audiences, framed with fictional dialogue that conveys her compelling influence upon writers ranging from Shakespeare to Aemilia Lanyer, Ben Jonson to Mary Wroth.

In *A Room of One's Own*, Virginia Woolf imagined that if Shakespeare had had a sister, equal in talent, she would have been 'so thwarted and hindered' that she could not have written her own poems and plays, let alone seen them published or performed (2004: 57). We now know that Woolf was wrong. Defying the era's constricting morals and mores, some women authors in Renaissance England found space and recognition – and with it, scandal and censure. Woolf didn't know about them, because over the years they had been erased from the 'canon' of accepted classics. My projected biofiction series *Shakespeare's Sisters*, which commences with *Imperfect Alchemist*, presents an array of early modern women authors as autonomous peers of Shakespeare, rather than simply as passive objects of desire or figures of inspiration. In six interrelated biofictional novels, the series aims to restore attention to these remarkable female figures – Mary Sidney Herbert, Mary Wroth, Amelia Lanyer, Anne Clifford, Elizabeth Cary, Queen Anna of Denmark – by capturing their stories from their own perspectives. *Shakespeare's Sisters* centres on women whose lives and voices both shape and are shaped by women, many of whom play a part not simply in Shakespeare's circle, but in each other's stories.

The only woman author from this group who has been treated in multiple biofictions is Amelia Lanyer, again most consistently represented as Shakespeare's 'dark lady'. The title of Mary Sharratt's novel *The Dark Lady's Mask: A Novel of Shakespeare's Muse* (2016) says it all. While a passionate and eloquent character in her own right, Sharratt's Lanier receives the most attention for her identity as the instrument of Shakespeare's invention. Nonetheless, in refreshing contrast to the handful of other novels that include Mary Sidney Herbert in a supporting role, Sharratt gives the Countess her due as the translator of Robert Garnier's *Marc Antoine* through a masque performance drawn from that translation in which Sharratt's Lanier performs (2016: 81). And toward the end of the novel, Mary Sidney Herbert sends Lanier her *Psalms* and affirms her admiration for Lanier's *Salve Deus Rex Judaeorum* (Ibid., 371).

Sharratt opens her historical afterword to the novel by affirming that 'this is a work of fiction. There is no historical evidence to prove that Aemilia Bassano Lanier was the Dark Lady of Shakespeare's sonnets' (Ibid., 394). She admits, however, that 'as a novelist I could not resist the allure of the Dark Lady mythos' (Ibid., 394). In this compelling fictional narrative, Sharratt's Lanier inspires and empowers Shakespeare's success, only to be abandoned and effectively repudiated by the playwright. And yet, after Shakespeare's death, Lanier receives a box of papers, densely packed, with a missive saying only 'For my eternal Muse.' Enclosed are all of Shakespeare's plays, including 'the early comedies that they had written together and that he had gone on to revise and make wholly his own, as if to erase her' (Ibid., 388). Reading the later plays, Lanier finds herself in Shakespeare's *Othello* as Emilia, who speaks 'lines so passionate, they might have come from her own *Salve Deus*', and recognizes her lost daughter, conceived with Will, in *The Winter's Tale*, where 'Odilia live[s] again in Perdita' (Ibid., 390). Although resolved to see these plays published with a preface by Ben Jonson 'to insure Will's posterity', she reflects that 'once more, men would be her mask and she would be erased. Yet she was the indelible thread woven into Will's great tapestry' (Ibid., 392). While Lanier's great religious poem, *Salve Deus Rex Judaeorum*, is described in the novel, the culmination of the narrative represents her central achievement as being Shakespeare's 'eternal Muse', the vital thread in his 'great tapestry'.

Another Shakespearean biofiction that sets out to celebrate Aemilia Lanyer is Morgan Lloyd Malcolm's play *Emilia*, which premiered to glowing reviews at Shakespeare's Globe in 2019 before transferring to the West End. This eloquent and bold transmutation of Aemilia Lanyer's voice offers much to admire, including its focus on Lanyer's identity as a poet, as well as its central attention, through casting preferences, to gender and colour as explicit topics. Once again, however, the focus on women's voices serves more to celebrate the brilliance of Shakespeare's characterizations of women, by attributing his genius to the formative influence of a woman such as Lanyer in his circle, than to celebrate the brilliance of the women themselves.

Here again, Mary Sidney Herbert appears as a supporting character who serves as an intermittent mentor to Emilia. Dismissing Shakespeare's writing as 'bilge', Malcolm's Countess introduces Emilia to Shakespeare, with the caveat that 'she's not your type' (2018: 20-21). The Countess declares that she will see her own poems published one day and encourages Emilia to do the same, advising her to 'play the game well Emilia and you will succeed' (Ibid., 20). That brief interaction marks the extent of the play's acknowledgement that Mary Sidney Herbert was a published author. What's more, Malcolm includes only one example of Aemilia Lanyer's actual published voice.

Malcolm shows Emilia constantly writing and asserting when discouraged that 'I will write my way out of this. No one can take my words from me. At least I have that' (Ibid., 45). And yet the majority of her speeches consist primarily of language adapted from Shakespeare's Emilia in *Othello* – most notably in complaining, 'have not we affections, desires for sport and frailty, as men have?' – so that the audience can accept Malcolm's fiction that Shakespeare stole such speeches from Emilia for his plays. When Emilia discovers that she has become known as the 'dark lady' of Shakespeare's sonnets, she laments that this is how she'll be remembered, exclaiming, 'Is there anything more violating?' (Ibid., 72). In Malcolm's play, Emilia's other writing is reduced to a reference to short poems with 'subtle warnings and instruction to women on how to approach marriage' (Ibid., 60), a fictional invention. The single moment when Malcolm accords Emilia her legitimate historical voice occurs near the end of the play, in the blistering language of Aemilia Lanyer's dedication of *Salve Deus Rex Judaeorum*, 'To the Vertuous Reader', excoriating men who 'do like Vipers deface the wombes wherein they were bred' (Ibid., 76).

Malcolm's play achieves an effective and moving dramatization of feminism, interleaving historical with modern women's voices onstage. However, the play perpetuates the practice of many modern biofictions, whether on page or stage, that represent female figures in Shakespeare's circle in the role of lover and/or muse. When biofictions choose to feature these women not through their own words but as figures imagined to have challenged, inspired, and deepened Shakespeare's characterizations of women, their own voices and perspectives are lost.

In *Strange Labyrinth,* my own sequel to *Imperfect Alchemist,* I focus on the story of Mary Wroth, England's first female fiction writer, struggling to create a place of her own in a world where most women's roles were scripted by men. Recognizing connections between the early modern and modern worlds, *Strange Labyrinth* delves into complex issues of race, gender, and sexual orientation in Jacobean England. My novel explores how Wroth, in her prose romance *Urania*, drew on her own experiences – as wife and widow, mother and lover, author and friend – to depict characters pursuing paths never previously represented by a woman in print.

My biofictional representation imagines an historically likely interaction between Wroth and Shakespeare on the grounds of Wilton House at the performance of *As You Like It* that is documented in the archival papers of the Countess of Pembroke and also occurs in *Imperfect Alchemist.* In *Strange Labyrinth,* a conversation with the playwright after the performance includes Mary's observation that 'breeches are only the start of liberty for women [...] and allowing Rosalind the last word was a nice gesture of possibility' (Miller forthcoming). Shakespeare then tells Mary, 'I've written something for you and your cousin,' and hands her the sonnet 'Let me not to the marriage of true minds', adding that 'the poem speaks for itself, and for those readers who may find their own truth within it' (Miller forthcoming). Later that evening Mary Wroth pens her own poem, 'As these drops fall', in response to Shakespeare's sonnet, which rings changes on the phrase 'love is not love' (Miller forthcoming).

My biofictional reconstruction of the interaction between Mary Wroth and William Shakespeare takes inspiration from Wroth scholars who have traced the formative presence of early modern women in Shakespeare's circle. Jane Kingsley-Smith advances a compelling argument that Shakespeare composed Sonnet 116 for 'the unique historical situation of the marriages of William Herbert, 3rd Earl of Pembroke and his cousin (who was also his mistress), Lady Mary Sidney,' who became Mary Wroth upon her marriage (2016: 292). Considering the further possibility that Wroth might have served as a patron to Shakespeare, Kingsley-Smith suggests that Wroth can be seen to function 'not as a Dark Lady but as a "Begetter"' (Ibid., 300). Advancing our modern awareness that early modern women such as Mary Sidney Herbert and Mary Wroth authored works that both engage with and diverge from the works of Shakespeare, *Strange Labyrinth* represents Mary Wroth performing the part of Cleopatra in her aunt's *Antonius* and subsequently staging a production of her own play at Penshurst Place. *Love's Victory* reconfigures Shakespeare's examples of same-sex friendship and heterosexual romantic love in a play such as *As You Like It* into an affirmation of a woman's right to choose, whether a male lover or the 'liberty' of chastity'.

I offer these examples of my own biofictional treatment of Mary Sidney Herbert's and Mary Wroth's interactions with Shakespeare because, unlike stage plays such as Mark Rylance's *I Am Shakespeare* and Morgan Lloyd Malcolm's *Emilia*, I am committed to bringing the actual voices of early modern women authors in Shakespeare's circle to the attention of modern audiences.

Interestingly, in many of the examples discussed in this essay, Shakespearean biofictions can be seen not so much as narrative explorations of the historical figure of Shakespeare as speculative inventions regarding how other historical figures, including women in his circle, might have shaped his plays. In some sense, then, recent Shakespearean biofictions that feature early modern women seem concerned less to celebrate these women's voices than to admire Shakespeare's female characters, whose creation they fictionally credit to the formative presence of women in Shakespeare's circle. An implicit assumption underlying these works is that Shakespeare must have had a female 'muse', or even collaborator, in order to be able to conceive such complex and convincing women characters. This notion serves as an adjunct to the authorship question.

Mark Rylance's play *I Am Shakespeare* revolves around that very question. It climaxes in an overlapping chorus of voices that includes Shakespeare scholars as well as Shakespeare's characters exploring 'who Shakespeare is' and 'who am I?'. The chorus culminates in an original sonnet about an oak tree, spoken in alternating lines by the four 'authors' represented in the play – the historical 'William Shakspar', Francis Bacon, Edward de Vere, and Lady Mary Sidney – that concludes that everyone owns the tree. The modern protagonist of the play, Frank Charlton, 'a Shakespearean authorship researcher who was once a star Shakespeare academic', asks, 'What's in a name? Suppose we all agreed upon the name, we'd still imagine many different Shakespeares'. In the final scene in the film *Spartacus,* where all the slaves stand up and claim to be Spartacus in order to hide and protect him (2012: 95), Frank finds his answer to the authorship controversy: 'He hid himself so that we could each be him. Our own author. Our own authority'. Thus when the constable who has been investigating the true identity of Shakespeare throughout the play returns to the stage, Frank, and his neighbour Barry – and, ideally, members of the audience – all rise to affirm 'I am Shakespeare' (Ibid., 93-97). As Rylance explains in his introduction, he is 'more concerned with the search for identity, our own identity, than the search for the identity of the author of the Shakespeare works' (Ibid., 7).

Indeed, I propose that many Shakespearean biofictions on page and stage are more concerned with enhancing audience appreciation of Shakespeare's plays through engagement with other historical figures than with exploring Shakespeare's 'true' identity. Thus the 'bio' in these biofictions finally turns out to reflect not simply the biographical details of historical figures, but also the lives and identities of modern playwrights and audiences, novelists and readers, who may find ourselves appreciating Shakespeare anew, not as icon so much as participant in our quests to make sense of our own worlds.

REFERENCES
A Discovery of Witches (2018-2022), [TV series] SkyOne.
Harkness, D. (2012), Shadow of Night, New York: Viking Penguin.
Kingsley-Smith, J. (2016), '"Let me not to the marriage of true minds": Shakespeare's Sonnet for Lady Mary Wroth', Shakespeare Survey, 69: 292-301.
Lamb, M. (2019), '"Love is not love": Shakespeare's Sonnet 116, Pembroke, and the Inns of Court', Shakespeare Quarterly, 70 (2): 101-128.
Lanier, D. (2002), Shakespeare and Modern Popular Culture, Oxford: Oxford University Press.
Lloyd Malcolm, M. (2018), Emilia, London: Oberon Books.
Miller, N. (2014), 'As She Likes It: Same-Sex Friendship and Romantic Love in Wroth and Shakespeare', in P. Salzman and M. Wynne-Davies (eds), Mary Wroth and Shakespeare, 137-50, London: Routledge.
Miller, N. (2020), Imperfect Alchemist, London: Allison & Busby Books.
Miller, N. (2022), Strange Labyrinth, unpublished manuscript [publication info forthcoming].
Rylance, M. (2012), I Am Shakespeare, London: Nick Hearn Books.
Sharratt, M. (2016), The Dark Lady's Mask: A Novel of Shakespeare's Muse, Boston: Houghton Mifflin.
Williams, R. (2012), Sweet Swan of Avon: Did a Woman Write Shakespeare?, Santa Fe, New Mexico: Wilton Circle Press.
Woods, S. (2022), 'Lanyer: The Dark Lady and the Shades of Fiction', in J. Fitzmaurice, N. J. Miller and S. J. Steen (eds), Authorizing Early Modern European Women: From Biography to Biofiction, Amsterdam: Amsterdam University Press.
Woolf, V. ([1929] 2004), A Room Of One's Own, London: Penguin.
Forthcoming in Shakespearean Biofiction on the Contemporary Stage and Screen, ed. Ronan Hatfull and Edel Semple. Bloomsbury Publishing, 2023.

I was born in Los Angeles, California, on a street named "Enchanted Way." I am descended on my mother's side from a Japanese shogun of the late 1500s and on my father's side from Dutch-English settlers who came to the American colonies in the Mayflower era. Being aware of what my ancestors were doing while Mary Sidney Herbert was alive has added resonance to the process of composing this novel. I wrote my first novel at the age of twelve – an 80-page hand-written mystery set in the England of Jane Austen and the Bronte sisters.

Captivated by Shakespeare and Renaissance England, I produced an undergraduate senior thesis at Princeton on the plays of Christopher Marlowe, and a doctoral dissertation at Harvard on the works of Sir Philip Sidney and his niece Lady Mary Wroth, the first woman to publish a sonnet sequence and a prose romance in Shakespeare's England. My first book, Changing the Subject, placed Wroth's writings in relation to other Renaissance women authors such as Sidney's sister, Mary Sidney Herbert – women whose writings brought women's lives to light and their voices to life.

I had four children before earning tenure at the University of Arizona, where I was diagnosed with multiple sclerosis at the age of forty. I have been guided in moving forward by the teachings of Thich Nhat Hahn in practicing mindfulness as a mother, author, teacher, and person of color.

I live in Northampton, Massachusetts, where I teach at Smith College on Shakespeare and "Shakespeare's Sisters." I am the recipient of the Sherrerd Award for Distinguished Teaching, and three of my previous books have received awards from the Society for the Study of Early Modern Women and Gender.

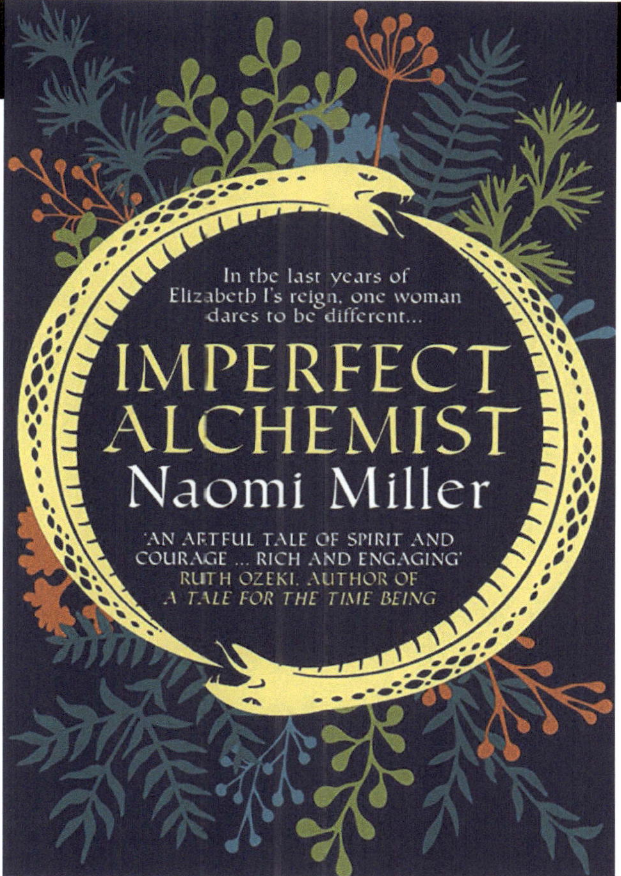

A remarkable life lost to history is brought into sharp focus

England, 1575. Young Mary Sidney is bearing a devastating loss while her father plans her alliance to Henry Herbert, Earl of Pembroke. But Mary is determined to make her mark on the world as a writer and scientist.

As Mary Sidney Herbert steps into her new life with the earl at his home, Wilton House, an unusual friendship is forged between her and servant Rose Commin, a country girl with a surprising artistic gift, that will change their lives for ever.

Defying the conventions of their time, mistress and maid will face the triumphs, revelations and dangers that lie ahead together.

'An artful tale of spirit and courage ... Rich and engaging' - Ruth Ozeki, author of *A Tale of the Time Being*

'A tribute to the strong women of the times ... I wholeheartedly recommend it' - Margaret George, author of *The Autobiography of Henry VIII*

THE GREAT SHAKESPEAREAN AUTHORSHIP DEBATE

Visit doubtaboutwill.org to learn more or to sign the "Declaration of Reasonable Doubt"

Famous Doubters:

HRH Prince Phillip
Mortimer J. Adler
Harry A. Blackmun
Chalie Chaplin
William Y. Elliot
Ralph Waldo Emerson
Clifton Fadiman
Sigmund Freud
John Galsworthy
Sir John Gielgud
Sir George Greenwood
Sir William Tyrone Guthrie

Henry James
William James
Paul H. Nitze
Henry John Temple, Lord Palmerston
Lewis F. Powell, Jr.
Hugh R. Trevor-Roper, Baron Dacre
Mark Twain
Orson Welles
Walt Whitman
Daphne du Maurier
Sir Derek Jacobi
Mark Rylance
Helen Keller
Malcolm X
Anne Rice
James Joyce
Benjamin Disraeli
Charles DeGaulle
Otto von Bismarck
David McCullough
Maxwell Perkins
Lincoln Schuster
Robin Williams
Samuel Taylor Coleridge
and Thomas Hardy;

among many others around the world and throughout history.

While definitive proof will never be known, the debate continues and continues to grow from strength to strength.

You can watch this debate between Sir Derek Jacobi and Mark Rylance on Youtube, delve into this mystery yourself, and draw your own conclusions. Needless to say, the premise for or against Shakespeare or any other candidate makes for a great foundation on which to base a historical fiction novel... as some writers have already dared to take the plunge.

https://youtu.be/7ZNYifQfYiE

THE BARD OF AVON
WILLIAM SHAKESPEARE

William Shakespeare (bapt. 26 April 1564 – 23 April 1616) was an English playwright, poet and actor. He is regarded as the greatest writer in the English language and the world's pre-eminent dramatist. He is often called England's national poet and the "Bard of Avon" (or simply "the Bard"). His extant works, including collaborations, consist of some 39 plays, 154 sonnets, three long narrative poems, and a few other verses, some of uncertain authorship. His plays have been translated into every major living language and are performed more often than those of any other playwright.[8] He remains arguably the most influential writer in the English language, and his works continue to be studied and reinterpreted.

Shakespeare was born and raised in Stratford-upon-Avon, Warwickshire. At the age of 18, he married Anne Hathaway, with whom he had three children: Susanna, and twins Hamnet and Judith. Sometime between 1585 and 1592, he began a successful career in London as an actor, writer, and part-owner of a playing company called the Lord Chamberlain's Men, later known as the King's Men. At age 49 (around 1613), he appears to have retired to Stratford, where he died three years later. Few records of Shakespeare's private life survive; this has stimulated considerable speculation about such matters as his physical appearance, his sexuality, his religious beliefs and whether the works attributed to him were written by others.

Shakespeare produced most of his known works between 1589 and 1613. His early plays were primarily comedies and histories and are regarded as some of the best works produced in these genres. He then wrote mainly tragedies until 1608, among them Hamlet, Romeo and Juliet, Othello, King Lear, and Macbeth, all considered to be among the finest works in the English language. In the last phase of his life, he wrote tragicomedies (also known as romances) and collaborated with other playwrights.

Many of Shakespeare's plays were published in editions of varying quality and accuracy in his lifetime. However, in 1623, John Heminges and Henry Condell, two fellow actors and friends of Shakespeare's, published a more definitive text known as the First Folio, a posthumous collected edition of Shakespeare's dramatic works that included all but two of his plays. Its Preface was a prescient poem by Ben Jonson, a former rival of Shakespeare, that hailed Shakespeare with the now famous epithet: "not of an age, but for all time".

Shakespeare was the son of John Shakespeare, an alderman and a successful glover (glove-maker) originally from Snitterfield in Warwickshire, and Mary Arden, the daughter of an affluent landowning family. He was born in Stratford-upon-Avon, where he was baptised on 26 April 1564. His date of birth is unknown, but is traditionally observed on 23 April, Saint George's Day. This date, which can be traced to William Oldys and George Steevens, has proved appealing to biographers because Shakespeare died on the same date in 1616. He was the third of eight children, and the eldest surviving son.

Although no attendance records for the period survive, most biographers agree that Shakespeare was probably educated at the King's New School in Stratford, a free school chartered in 1553, about a quarter-mile (400 m) from his home. Grammar schools varied in quality during the Elizabethan era, but grammar school curricula were largely similar: the basic Latin text was standardised by royal decree, and the school would have provided an intensive education in grammar based upon Latin classical authors.

At the age of 18, Shakespeare married 26-year-old Anne Hathaway. The consistory court of the Diocese of Worcester issued a marriage licence on 27 November 1582. The next day, two of Hathaway's neighbours posted bonds guaranteeing that no lawful claims impeded the marriage. The ceremony may have been arranged in some haste since the Worcester chancellor allowed the marriage banns to be read once instead of the usual three times, and six months after the marriage Anne gave birth to a daughter, Susanna, baptised 26 May 1583. Twins, son Hamnet and daughter Judith, followed almost two years later and were baptised 2 February

1585. Hamnet died of unknown causes at the age of 11 and was buried 11 August 1596.

Shakespeare's coat of arms, from the 1602 book The book of coates and creasts. Promptuarium armorum. It features spears as a pun on the family name.

After the birth of the twins, Shakespeare left few historical traces until he is mentioned as part of the London theatre scene in 1592. The exception is the appearance of his name in the "complaints bill" of a law case before the Queen's Bench court at Westminster dated Michaelmas Term 1588 and 9 October 1589. Scholars refer to the years between 1585 and 1592 as Shakespeare's "lost years". Biographers attempting to account for this period have reported many apocryphal stories. Nicholas Rowe, Shakespeare's first biographer, recounted a Stratford legend that Shakespeare fled the town for London to escape prosecution for deer poaching in the estate of local squire Thomas Lucy. Shakespeare is also supposed to have taken his revenge on Lucy by writing a scurrilous ballad about him. Another 18th-century story has Shakespeare starting his theatrical career minding the horses of theatre patrons in London. John Aubrey reported that Shakespeare had been a country schoolmaster. Some 20th-century scholars suggested that Shakespeare may have been employed as a schoolmaster by Alexander Hoghton of Lancashire, a Catholic landowner who named a certain "William Shakeshafte" in his will. Little evidence substantiates such stories other than hearsay collected after his death, and Shakeshafte was a common name in the Lancashire area.

It is not known definitively when Shakespeare began writing, but contemporary allusions and records of performances show that several of his plays were on the London stage by 1592. By then, he was sufficiently known in London to be attacked in print by the playwright Robert Greene in his Groats-Worth of Wit:

... there is an upstart Crow, beautified with our feathers, that with his Tiger's heart wrapped in a Player's hide, supposes he is as well able to bombast out a blank verse as the best of you: and being an absolute Johannes factotum, is in his own conceit the only Shake-scene in a country.

Scholars differ on the exact meaning of Greene's words, but most agree that Greene was accusing Shakespeare of reaching above his rank in trying to match such university-educated writers as Christopher Marlowe, Thomas Nashe, and Greene himself (the so-called "University Wits"). The italicised phrase parodying the line "Oh, tiger's heart wrapped in a woman's hide" from Shakespeare's Henry VI, Part 3, along with the pun "Shake-scene", clearly identify Shakespeare as Greene's target. As used here, Johannes Factotum ("Jack of all trades") refers to a second-rate tinkerer with the work of others, rather than the more common "universal genius".

Greene's attack is the earliest surviving mention of Shakespeare's work in the theatre. Biographers suggest that his career may have begun any time from the mid-1580s to just before Greene's remarks. After 1594, Shakespeare's plays were performed only by the Lord Chamberlain's Men, a company owned by a group of players, including Shakespeare, that soon became the leading playing company in London. After the death of Queen Elizabeth in 1603, the company was awarded a royal patent by the new King James I, and changed its name to the King's Men.

In 1599, a partnership of members of the company built their own theatre on the south bank of the River Thames, which they named the Globe. In 1608, the partnership also took over the Blackfriars indoor theatre. Extant records of Shakespeare's property purchases and investments indicate that his association with the company made him a wealthy man, and in 1597, he bought the second-largest house in Stratford, New Place, and in 1605, invested in a share of the parish tithes in Stratford.

Some of Shakespeare's plays were published in quarto editions, beginning in 1594, and by 1598, his name had become a selling point and began to appear on the title pages. Shakespeare continued to act in his own and other plays after his success as a playwright. The 1616 edition of Ben Jonson's Works names him on the cast lists for Every Man in His Humour (1598) and Sejanus His Fall (1603). The absence of his name from the 1605 cast list for Jonson's Volpone is taken by some scholars as a sign that his acting career was nearing its end. The First Folio of 1623, however, lists Shakespeare as one of "the Principal Actors in all these Plays", some of which were first staged after Volpone, although one cannot know for certain which roles he played. In 1610, John Davies of Hereford wrote that "good Will" played "kingly" roles. In 1709, Rowe passed down a tradition that Shakespeare played the ghost of Hamlet's father. Later traditions maintain that he also played Adam in As You Like It, and the Chorus in Henry V, though scholars doubt the sources of that information.

Throughout his career, Shakespeare divided his time between London and Stratford. In 1596, the year before he bought New Place as his family home in Stratford, Shakespeare was living in the parish of St. Helen's, Bishopsgate, north of the River Thames. He moved across the river to Southwark by 1599, the same year his company constructed the Globe Theatre there.[64][66] By 1604, he had moved north of the river again, to an area north of St Paul's Cathedral with many fine houses. There, he rented rooms from a French Huguenot named Christopher Mountjoy, a maker of women's wigs and other headgear.

Nicholas Rowe was the first biographer to record the tradition, repeated by Samuel Johnson, that Shakespeare retired to Stratford "some years before his death". He was still working as an actor in London in 1608; in an answer to the sharers' petition in 1635, Cuthbert Burbage stated that after purchasing the lease of the Blackfriars Theatre in 1608 from Henry Evans, the King's Men "placed men players" there, "which were Heminges, Condell, Shakespeare, etc.". However, it is perhaps relevant that the bubonic plague raged in London throughout 1609. The London public playhouses were repeatedly closed during extended outbreaks of the plague (a total of over 60 months closure between May 1603 and February 1610 which meant there was often no acting work. Retirement from all work was uncommon at that time. Shakespeare continued to visit London during the years 1611–1614. In 1612, he was called as a witness in Bellott v Mountjoy, a court case concerning the marriage settlement of Mountjoy's daughter, Mary. In March 1613, he bought a gatehouse in the former Blackfriars priory; and from November 1614, he was in London for several weeks with his son-in-law, John Hall. After 1610, Shakespeare wrote fewer plays, and none are attributed to him after 1613. His last three plays were collaborations, probably with John Fletcher, who succeeded him as the house playwright of the King's Men. He retired in 1613, before the Globe Theatre burned down during the performance of Henry VIII on 29 June.

Shakespeare died on 23 April 1616, at the age of 52. He died within a month of signing his will, a document which he begins by describing himself as being in "perfect health". No extant contemporary source explains how or why he died. Half a century later, John Ward, the vicar of Stratford, wrote in his notebook: "Shakespeare, Drayton, and Ben Jonson had a merry meeting and, it seems, drank too hard, for Shakespeare died of a fever there contracted", not an impossible scenario since Shakespeare knew Jonson and Drayton. Of the tributes from fellow authors, one refers to his relatively sudden death: "We wondered, Shakespeare, that thou went'st so soon / From the world's stage to the grave's tiring room."

He was survived by his wife and two daughters. Susanna had married a physician, John Hall, in 1607, and Judith had married Thomas Quiney, a vintner, two months before Shakespeare's death. Shakespeare signed his last will and testament on 25 March 1616; the following day, his new son-in-law, Thomas Quiney was found guilty of fathering an illegitimate son by Margaret Wheeler, who had died during childbirth. Thomas was ordered by the church court to do public penance, which would have caused much shame and embarrassment for the Shakespeare family.

Shakespeare bequeathed the bulk of his large estate to his elder daughter Susanna under stipulations that she pass it down intact to "the first son of her body". The Quineys had three children, all of whom died without marrying. The Halls had one child, Elizabeth, who married twice but died without children in 1670, ending Shakespeare's direct line. Shakespeare's will scarcely mentions his wife, Anne, who was probably entitled to one-third of his estate automatically. He did make a point, however, of leaving her "my second best bed", a bequest that has led to much speculation. Some scholars see the bequest as an insult to Anne, whereas others believe that the second-best bed would have been the matrimonial bed and therefore rich in significance.

Shakespeare was buried in the chancel of the Holy Trinity Church two days after his death. The epitaph carved into the stone slab covering his grave includes a curse against moving his bones, which was carefully avoided during restoration of the church in 2008:

Good friend, for Jesus' sake forbear,
To dig the dust enclosed here.
Blessed be the man that spares these stones,
And cursed be he that moves my bones.

Some time before 1623, a funerary monument was erected in his memory on the north wall, with a half-effigy of him in the act of writing. Its plaque compares him to Nestor, Socrates, and Virgil. In 1623, in conjunction with the publication of the First Folio, the Droeshout engraving was published. Shakespeare has been commemorated in many statues and memorials around the world, including funeral monuments in Southwark Cathedral and Poets' Corner in Westminster Abbey..

Info from Wikipedia. Images from Deposit Photos / Shutterstock

THE ART OF DRESSING LIKE A QUEEN

JUDITH ARNOPP

I've always loved medieval and Tudor history, so it made sense to set my books in that era. Once I had a few novels under my belt I began to attend events, selling my books from a small trader tent, meeting readers and making friends in the re-enactment world. Wanting to blend in, my husband and I dressed up in Tudor gear and had the time of our lives! It was like a dream come true to find myself surrounded by armoured knights, nobles and commoners, to see the 16th century crafts and lifestyles. I knew within the first half hour that I would be back the following year.

My very first outfit was so inaccurate I blush to think of it now but as soon as I was able I purchased a second-hand gown made by Gina Clark. It was such a gorgeous gown, and I am still disappointed that I got too fat for it. The cost if a new one is considerable, and I wanted to own clothing from different status and eras. There was only one thing for it and never

one to know my limitations, armed with just school level sewing skills I decided to make my own.

My first attempt was laughable but luckily I made it from an old pair of curtains – curtains I quickly realised were far too small for the purpose. Undaunted, I bought more fabric and began again with better results this time, but it wasn't until my third gown that I finally came up with a wearable garment. I also started to make my husband's clothes. He now has almost as many different outfits as me. Then I made a set of clothes for Henry VIII and dragged my son along to play the part of the king. Unfortunately, he can't come out with us very often but when he does, he makes the perfect king.

Before long I'd met a fellow Tudor enthusiast who was keen to join me and we started a small group, The Fyne Companye of Cambria, and now in the summer we haunt the castles of West Wales. There are four

main members now with others who come out with us when they can. We don't take ourselves very seriously; we believe re-enactment should be fun and if our costumes are not quite right, they are close enough to convince the visitors to the castles. We enjoy adding to their experience and sometimes the caste throws in a free lunch – what could be better than that?

My first few projects were daunting, but I learned quickly and am still learning. I will never be an expert, but the most important lesson was not to be afraid of it. I now know how to construct a stiffened bodice, how to pleat miles and miles of skirt into a tiny (well, it seems tiny) waistband. My methods are not always authentic, but I manage to produce French hoods, gabled hoods, coifs, and bags for fellow re-enactors and have also sewn a couple of medieval houppelande gowns, shifts and kirtles, and several more Tudor gowns. I am not and never will rank among the best sewers, but it didn't stop Pen and Sword publishing from approaching me to write a book about Tudor fashion. I did explain that there are far more accomplished historical sewers out there, but I hope to illustrate in the book that will be published in September 2023 that with research, patience, determination and sometimes a little bit of cheating, anyone can dress like a Tudor.

Author Biography

A lifelong history enthusiast and avid reader, Judith holds a BA in English/Creative writing and an MA in Medieval Studies. She lives on the coast of West Wales where she writes both fiction and non-fiction. She is best known for her novels set in the Medieval and Tudor period, focussing on the perspective of historical women but recently she has been writing from the perspective of Henry VIII himself.

Judith is also a founder member of a re-enactment group called The Fyne Companye of Cambria which is when she began to experiment with sewing historical garments. She now makes clothes and accessories both for the group and others. She is not a professionally trained sewer but through trial, error and determination has learned how to make authentic looking, if not strictly historically accurate clothing. She is currently working on a non-fiction book about Tudor clothing which will be published by Pen and Sword.

Images provided by Judith Arnopp

Her novels include

:

A Song of Sixpence: the story of Elizabeth of York

The Beaufort Chronicle: the life of Lady Margaret Beaufort (three book series)

A Matter of Conscience: Henry VIII, the Aragon Years (Book one of The Henrician Chronicle)

A Matter of Faith: Henry VIII, the days of the Phoenix (Book two of The Henrician Chronicle)

A Matter of Time: Henry VIII, the Dying of the Light (coming soon)

The Kiss of the Concubine: a story of Anne Boleyn

The Winchester Goose: at the court of Henry VIII

Intractable Heart: the story of Katheryn Parr

Sisters of Arden: on the Pilgrimage of Grace

The Heretic Wind: the life of Mary Tudor, Queen of England

Peaceweaver

The Forest Dwellers

The Song of Heledd

Webpage: <u>judithmarnopp.com</u>
Books: <u>author.to/juditharnoppbooks</u>
Blog: www.juditharnoppnovelist.blogspot.co.uk/

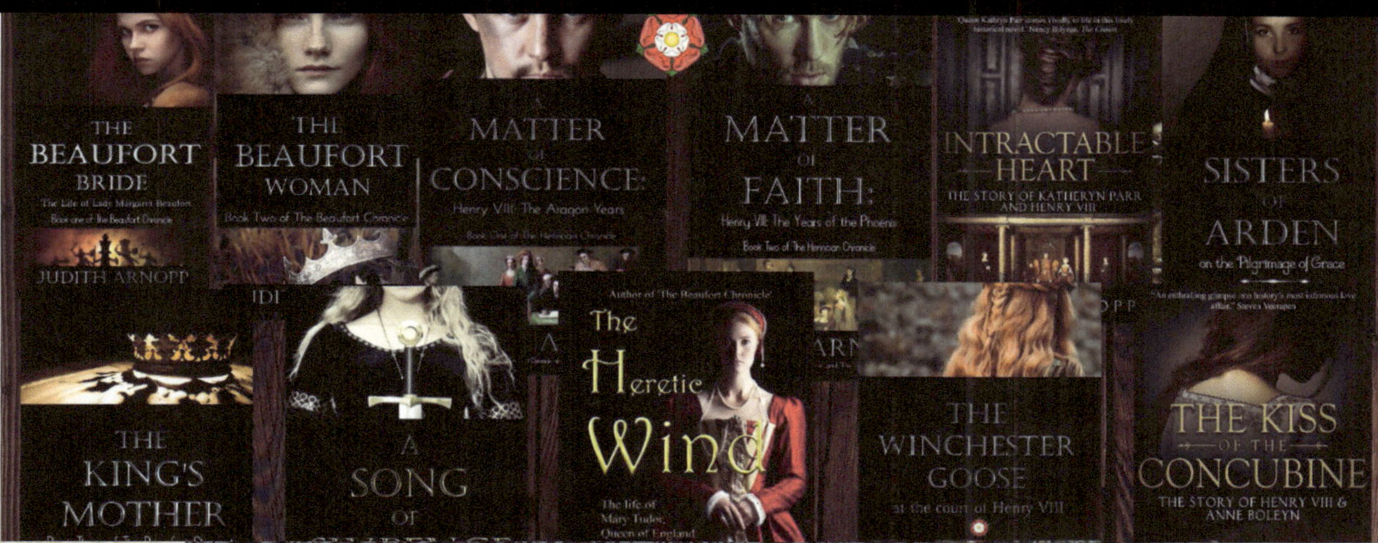

A lifelong history enthusiast and avid reader, Judith holds a BA in English/Creative writing and an MA in Medieval Studies. She lives on the coast of West Wales where she writes both fiction and non-fiction. She is best known for her novels set in the Medieval and Tudor period, focusing on the perspective of historical women but recently she has been writing from the perspective of Henry VIII himself.

Judith is also a founder member of a re-enactment group called The Fyne Companye of Cambria which is when she began to experiment with sewing historical garments. She now makes clothes and accessories both for the group and others. She is not a professionally trained sewer but through trial, error and determination has learned how to make authentic looking, if not strictly historically accurate clothing.

Jacket Design: Paul Wilkinson

For a complete list of current titles ring or write to:

PEN & SWORD BOOKS LIMITED
47 Church Street, Barnsley South Yorkshire S70 2AS
E-mail: enquiries@pen-and-sword.co.uk

Tel: 01226 734222
Or visit our website at:
www.pen-and-sword.co.uk

PEN & SWORD BOOKS (US)
1950 Lawrence Rd, Havertown, PA, 19083, USA
E-mail: Uspen-and-sword@casematepublishers.com

Tel: +1 601 853 9131
Or visit our website at:
www.penandswordbooks.com

OVER 7000 TITLES AVAILABLE.

A HOW-TO GUIDE FOR DRESSING LIKE A TUDOR.

Based on the author's own experience as a member of a re-enactment group, it offers tips and tricks on how to create your own historic garments.

This book traces the transition of fashion through the Tudor period from styles at court to the garments of ordinary folk.

UK £??.?? • US $??.??

HOW TO DRESS LIKE A TUDOR

JUDITH ARNOPP

Have you ever hankered to dress like a Tudor lord or lady, or perhaps you prefer the status of goodwife, or costermonger, or even a bawd?

For beginner historical reenactors, the path to authenticity can be bewildering and sometimes intimidating. Judith Arnopp uses her own experience, both as a historian and a medieval/Tudor lady, to make your own journey a little easier.

The author traces the transition of fashion from the relatively subtle styles popular at the court of Henry VII, through the carefully constructed royal grandeur of Henry VIII, Edward VI, and Mary I to the pinnacle of majesty and splendid iconography of Elizabeth I.

In contrast to the magnificence of court came the ordinary folk who, subject to sumptuary laws and regulations, wore garments of a simpler cut and cloth – a strata of society that formed the back bone of Tudor England.

This brief history of sixteenth century fashion examines clothing for both rich and poor, adult and child, and offers tips and tricks on how to begin to sew your first historically inspired garment, this book is aimed at helping the beginner learn How to Dress like a Tudor.

UK £??.??
US $??.??

www.pen-and-sword.co.uk

The King's Story.

Henry VIII, in his own words

'Superbly inventive insight into the mind of one of our most famous monarchs' –
Deborah Swift, author of the Italian Renaissance Series

#Kindle #Paperback

A MATTER OF CONSCIENCE:
Henry VIII: The Aragon Years
Book One of The Henrician Chronicle
JUDITH ARNOPP
Author of The Beaufort Chronicle and The Heretic Wind

A MATTER OF FAITH:
Henry VIII: The Years of the Phoenix
Book Two of The Henrician Chronicle
JUDITH ARNOPP
Author of The Beaufort Chronicle and The Heretic Wind

HER MAJESTY'S

SECRET SERVICE

The Enigmatic Spies of Queen Elizabeth I:
Unveiling the Secrets of Francis Walsingham and
Her Majesty's Spy Network

Queen Elizabeth I of England is widely celebrated as one of the most influential monarchs in history. Her reign, known as the Elizabethan era, witnessed a cultural and intellectual renaissance that transformed England into a global power. Amidst the political intrigues and religious conflicts of the time, Queen Elizabeth I's secret service and spy network played a crucial role in safeguarding her rule and protecting the realm. At the heart of this clandestine web was the enigmatic figure of Sir Francis Walsingham, a trusted advisor to the queen. In this blog post, we will explore the fascinating world of Queen Elizabeth I's secret service and delve into the remarkable achievements of Francis Walsingham and his network of spies.

The Threats Faced by Queen Elizabeth I

Queen Elizabeth I ascended to the throne in 1558, inheriting a realm plagued by internal and external challenges. As a Protestant queen in a predominantly Catholic Europe, Elizabeth faced the constant threat of assassination and invasion from Catholic powers, including Spain and France. Moreover, there were numerous domestic conspiracies to overthrow her rule, with various factions plotting to replace her with Mary, Queen of Scots or other claimants to the throne. To counter these threats, Elizabeth and her trusted advisor, Francis Walsingham, established an elaborate spy network.

Francis Walsingham: The Spymaster Extraordinaire

Sir Francis Walsingham, born in 1532, was a highly educated and shrewd diplomat who served as the principal secretary to Queen Elizabeth I. Recognizing the importance of intelligence gathering, Walsingham played a pivotal role in establishing a sophisticated spy network. His commitment to Queen and country was unwavering, and he spared no effort in rooting out potential conspiracies against the queen's life and authority.

The Role of Spies

Walsingham's spies, known as intelligencers, operated both domestically and internationally, providing the queen with critical information about potential threats. These agents were often skilled linguists, codebreakers, and masters of disguise. They infiltrated Catholic circles, diplomatic missions, and even foreign courts to gather information and thwart plots against Elizabeth's life. By exploiting their networks, Walsingham's spies provided the queen with invaluable intelligence that helped maintain her security.

Cracking Codes and Intercepting Messages

In an era when written communication was the primary means of conveying information, intercepting and deciphering coded messages became a crucial aspect of Walsingham's intelligence operations. To this end, he employed experts in cryptography who were adept at decoding secret correspondences. Through their efforts, Walsingham was able to gather critical insights into the plans of Elizabeth's enemies, enabling him to counteract their strategies effectively.

The Babington Plot and the Downfall of Mary, Queen of Scots

One of the most notorious threats to Queen Elizabeth I's reign was the Babington Plot, a conspiracy to assassinate the queen and replace her with Mary, Queen of Scots. Walsingham's spies infiltrated the conspiracy, and with their help, he obtained incriminating letters written by Mary, Queen of Scots, which revealed her involvement in the plot. These letters, when presented as evidence, sealed Mary's fate and ultimately led to her execution in 1587.

Espionage Techniques and Counterintelligence

Walsingham's spy network employed various espionage techniques to protect the queen and gather information. Agents used invisible inks, concealed messages in innocuous objects, and relied on secret codes to communicate. They utilized a range of disguises to maintain their cover and operated covertly in foreign territories. Walsingham also established a comprehensive system of counterintelligence, employing double agents to mislead and confound Elizabeth's enemies.

In the annals of espionage, few names resonate as strongly as Sir Francis Walsingham, the influential spymaster and statesman who served as the principal secretary to Queen Elizabeth I of England. Walsingham's spy network was renowned for its efficiency and effectiveness, employing various methods to gather intelligence and protect the crown. Among his many ingenious strategies was the utilization of young boys as spies, a tactic that proved instrumental in securing vital information during a tumultuous era.

During the late 16th century, England found itself beset by both internal and external threats. Queen Elizabeth's Protestant regime faced formidable adversaries, including Catholic powers such as Spain, France, and the Papal States, all of whom sought to destabilize the English monarchy and restore Catholicism. In this environment, Sir Francis Walsingham recognized the need for an efficient intelligence apparatus to safeguard the crown and counteract conspiracies.

Walsingham's efforts to build an extensive spy network involved a range of methods, including code-breaking, informants, and covert operations. However, one of his most distinctive approaches was the recruitment and deployment of young boys as spies. These boys, often orphans or from disadvantaged backgrounds, were considered inconspicuous and were readily able to infiltrate various social circles without arousing suspicion.

Role of Young Boy Spies

Walsingham's use of young boys as spies was shrewdly calculated. Boys were chosen for their perceived innocence, lack of political affiliations, and their ability to blend into different social settings. They were groomed to become informants, couriers, and observers, tasked with infiltrating influential households, taverns, and social gatherings where plots against the crown were hatched and discussed.

These young spies played an integral role in gathering critical information. They listened, observed, and reported back to their handlers, relaying conversations, plans, and movements of potential threats. Their unassuming presence allowed them to elicit candid discussions, gaining insights that might have eluded adult spies. Walsingham's network effectively transformed these boys into invaluable sources of intelligence, helping to foil numerous plots and safeguard the realm.

To prepare these young spies for their delicate tasks, Walsingham and his agents provided them with rigorous training. They were schooled in the art of deception, taught to read and write in code, and trained in basic espionage techniques. Their training encompassed developing an acute sense of observation, mastering the art of eavesdropping, and learning to blend in seamlessly with their surroundings.

The boys were also given specific roles, based on their individual strengths and circumstances. Some would act as messengers, discreetly passing information between agents and safe houses. Others would pose as servants, gaining access to the inner workings of influential households. Regardless of their assignments, these young spies were made aware of the gravity of their roles, understanding that their actions could shape the fate of the nation.

Sir Francis Walsingham's use of young boys as spies left an indelible mark on the history of espionage. His innovative approach not only expanded the capabilities of his spy network but also demonstrated the audacity and resourcefulness of his methods. The success of these boy spies can be attributed to the dedication and training provided by Walsingham's agents, as well as the resilience and courage of the boys themselves.

However, it is essential to acknowledge the ethical concerns surrounding the employment of child spies. The use of young boys, some as young as ten years old, raises questions about their welfare, vulnerability, and potential long-term psychological impact. While Walsingham's intentions were rooted in safeguarding the realm, the exploitation of children for intelligence purposes remains a contentious aspect of his legacy.

Sir Francis Walsingham's spy network was a formidable force in Elizabethan England, protecting the realm from numerous threats. The utilization of young boys as spies stands as a testament to Walsingham's ingenuity and the lengths he was willing to go to protect Queen Elizabeth I and her Protestant regime. While the practice of employing child spies is ethically contentious, it remains a notable chapter in the history of espionage, underscoring the sacrifices and unconventional tactics employed in the pursuit of national security.

The Spanish Armada: A Triumph of Intelligence

Perhaps the most significant testament to the effectiveness of Walsingham's secret service was the defeat of the Spanish Armada in 1588. The spy network, through its intricate web of informants, intercepted and decrypted messages that revealed the Spanish King Philip II's plans for the invasion of England. This intelligence allowed the English fleet, under the command of Sir Francis Drake and Lord Charles Howard, to anticipate and prepare for the attack. The subsequent victory over the Armada marked a turning point in European history and solidified England's status as a dominant naval power.

Legacy and Significance

The legacy of Queen Elizabeth I's secret service and spy network, orchestrated by Francis Walsingham, cannot be overstated. Their efforts preserved the queen's reign, thwarted numerous plots against her, and safeguarded England's security. By establishing a formidable intelligence apparatus, Walsingham set the stage for the development of modern intelligence agencies, laying the foundation for future spymasters and their networks.

Queen Elizabeth I's secret service and spy network, led by the remarkable Francis Walsingham, played a crucial role in protecting the queen, safeguarding the realm, and countering foreign threats during the Elizabethan era. Through their tireless efforts, these spies operated in the shadows, gathering intelligence, decoding messages, and preventing countless conspiracies against the queen. The achievements of Walsingham's network, especially in defeating the Spanish Armada, resonate through history and highlight the enduring significance of intelligence and espionage in the preservation of power and security.

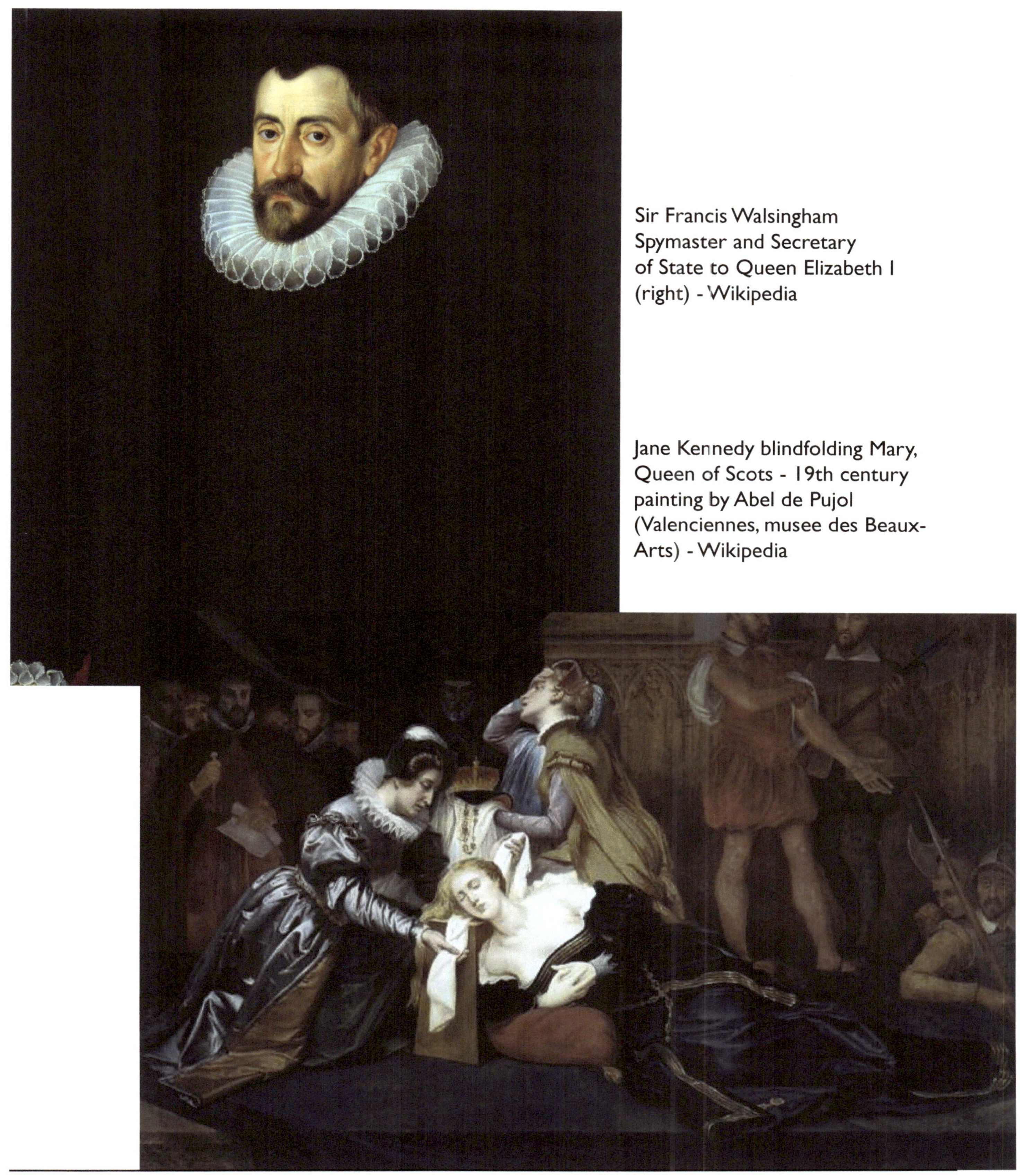

Sir Francis Walsingham Spymaster and Secretary of State to Queen Elizabeth I (right) - Wikipedia

Jane Kennedy blindfolding Mary, Queen of Scots - 19th century painting by Abel de Pujol (Valenciennes, musee des Beaux-Arts) - Wikipedia

HISTORIUM PRESS

BST. 2022

Purveyors of Fine Historical Fiction

"History in the Making"

THE HISTORIUM PRESS CATALOGUE

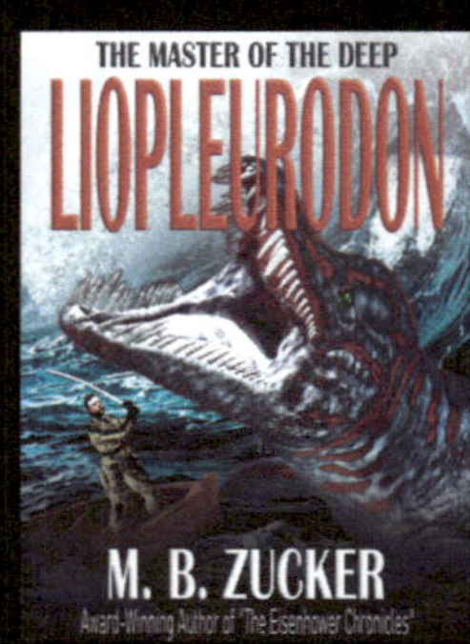

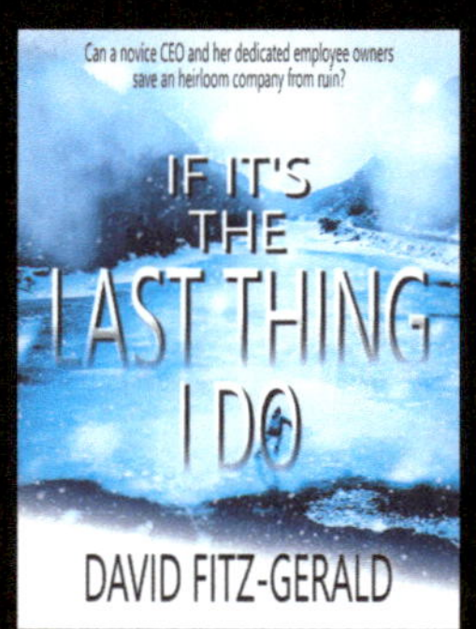

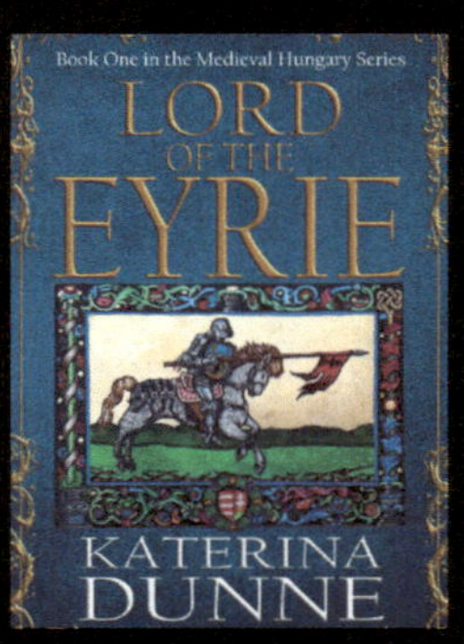

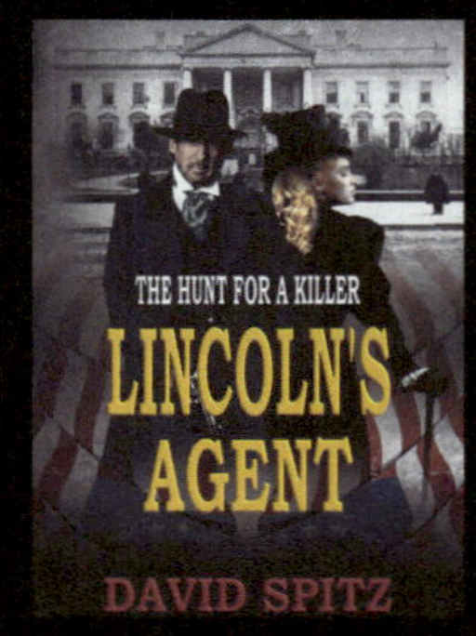

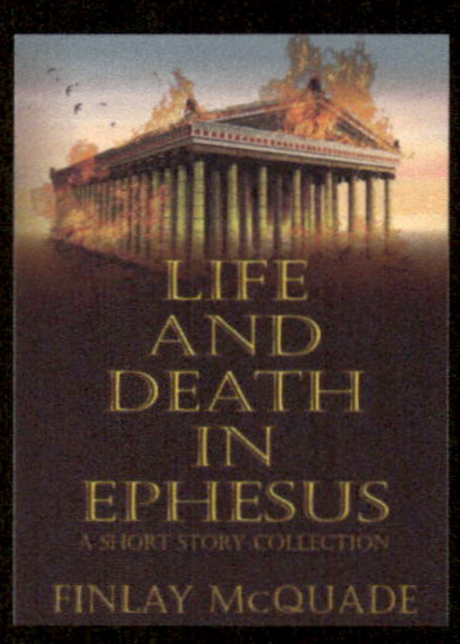

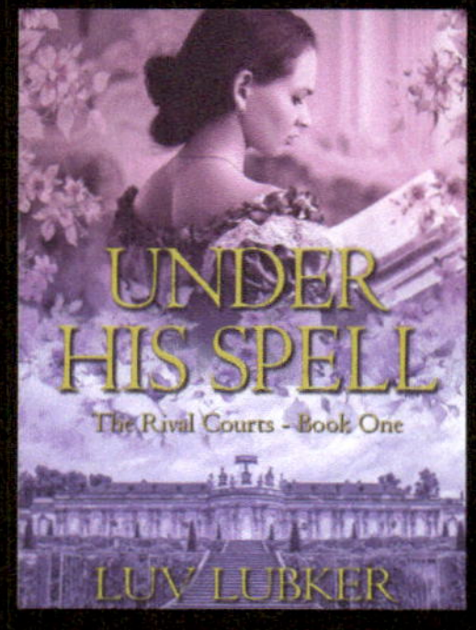

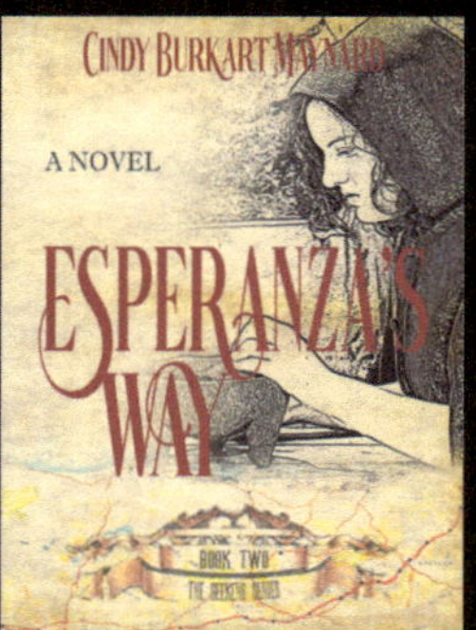

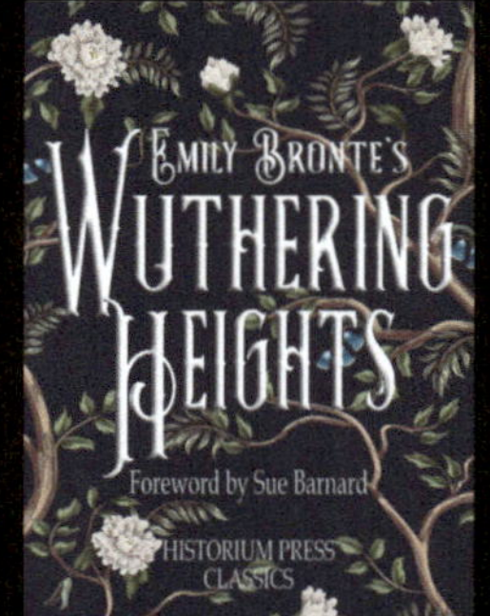

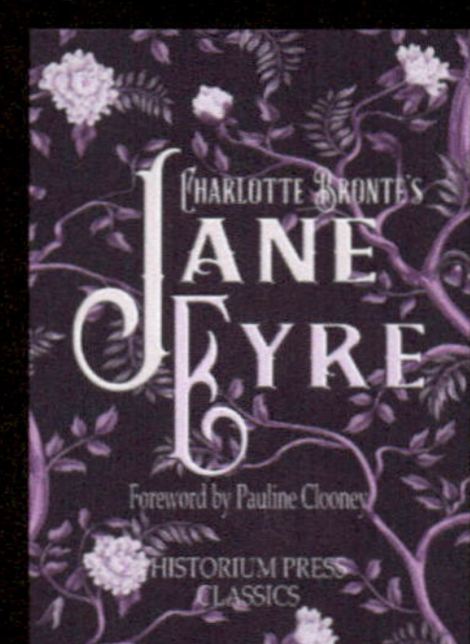

NOW ACCEPTING MANUSCRIPT SUBMISSIONS!

Visit www.historiumpress.com
or submit to historiumpublisher@gmail.com

Recipes Through the Ages

Tudor

Old Elizabethan Recipe for Chicken Pie

Make your Paste with cold Cream, Flour, Butter and the yolk of an Egg, roul it
very thin, and lay it in your Baking-pan, then lay Butter in the Bottom. Then lay
in your Chickens cut in quarters with some whole Mace, and Nutmeg sliced,
with some Marrow, hard Lettuce, Eryngo Root, and Citron Pill, with a few Dates
stoned and sliced: Then lay good store of Butter.

Close up your Pie and Bake it: Then Cut it open, and put in some Wine, Butter,
and Sugar with the Yolks of two or three Eggs well beaten together over the fire,
till it be thick, so serve it to the Table, and garnish your Dish with some pretty
Conceits made in Paste.

New Similar Recipe for Chicken Pie

FOR POACHING THE CHICKEN:
1 small onion
1 small leek
1 celery stalk
1 small carrot
4 chicken drumsticks
4 chicken thighs
1 bay leaf
a sprig of thyme
1.25 litres light chicken stock (or water)
500g block all-butter puff pastry
1 egg yolk, beaten with a little water, to glaze

FOR THE PIE FILLING:
2 medium carrots, peeled and cut on the diagonal into 1cm slices
2 medium leeks, trimmed and cut into 2cm slices
50g butter
50g plain flour, plus extra for dusting
2 tbsp single or double cream

Roughly chop the onion, leek, celery and carrot. Put the chicken in a wide pan with the vegetables, a level
teaspoon of salt and the bay leaf and thyme. Add enough stock just to cover the contents and bring gently
to the boil. Skim off any scum, reduce the heat, cover with a lid and poach the chicken for about 30 minutes or until the flesh feels tender when pierced with a knife and the juices run clear. Leave to cool in the
stock.
Melt the butter in another pan, stir in the flour and cook for a few minutes, stirring constantly, to make
a roux. Add a small ladleful of the hot stock, stirring well with a wooden spoon or balloon whisk. Repeat,
stirring all the time, until all the stock has been added. Season and stir in the cream, if using. Pour the
sauce over the chicken and veg and give it a stir. Leave to cool. Preheat the oven to 220°C, fan 200°C, gas
7.

On a floured surface, roll out the pastry to about ½cm thick, enough to generously cover the pie dish with an overlap. Butter the edge of the dish, cut a strip of pastry 2½cm wide from around the outside of the rolled-out pastry and press firmly round the edge of the dish. Brush with cold water and place the rest of the pastry on top, firming down the edge. Trim away any excess with a sharp knife. Crimp the edge with a fork and decorate the top with leaves or another design made from the pastry trimmings. Use a dab of water to make the bits stick.

Brush the pie with the beaten egg. Bake for 45-50 minutes until golden and bubbling hot.

When the chicken is cool enough to handle, strain off but reserve the stock (keep this for making the sauce) and discard the vegetables. Remove the skin from the chicken and discard. Pull all the meat from the bones and transfer to a 1.2 litre pie dish.

Bring 600ml of the reserved stock to the boil, add the carrots and simmer for 5 minutes. Add the leeks and, as soon as they come back to the boil, remove all the veg with a slotted spoon and add to the chicken.

Old Elizabethan Recipe for Banbury Cakes

Make a Posset of Sack and Cream, then take a Peck of fine Flour, half an Ounce of Mace, as much of Nutmeg, as much of Cinamon, beat them and searce them, two pounds of Butter, ten Eggs, leaving out half their Whites, one Pint and half of Ale-Yest, beat your Eggs very well, and strain them, then put your Yest, and some of the Posset to the Flour.

Stir them together, and put in your Butter cold in little pieces, but your Posset must be scalding hot; make it into a Paste, and let it lie one hour in a warm Cloth to rise, then put in ten pounds of Currans washed and dried very well, a little Musk and Ambergreece dissolved in Rosewater, put in a little Sugar among your Currans break your Paste into little pieces, when you go to put in your Currans, then lay a Lay of broken Paste, and then a Lay of Currans till all be in, then mingle your Paste and Currans well together, and keep out a little of your Paste in a warm Cloth to cover the top and bottom of your Cake, you must rowl the Cover very thin, and also the Bottom, and close them together over the Cake with a little Rosewater; prick the top and bottom with a small Pin or Needle.

When it is ready to go into the Oven, cut in the sides round about, let it stand two hours, then Ice it over with Rosewater or Orange Flour and Sugar, and the White of an Egg, and harden it in the Oven.

EASY BANBURY CAKES

1 package puff pastry* thawed
1 cup currants
1/4 cup unsalted butter
1/2 cup mixed candied peel
1/2 tsp. cinnamon
1/2 tsp. nutmeg
1/2 cup brown sugar
1 tbsp. port, sherry or rum
1 large egg white beaten
3 tbsp. caster sugar

Melt the butter and brown sugar, and add the dried fruit, spices, and port in a small saucepan. Let cool. Preheat your oven to 450F and line a baking sheet with parchment paper or a baking sheet. Roll out the pastry on a floured board ensuring a thickness of 1/4 inch. Cut two lines across and 2 lines down to make 9 squares.
Place a tablespoon of the fruit filling in each square. Wet the edges of each square with water and bring the edges together to seal. Turn each bundle over, and shape it into an oval.
Dip each cake into the beaten egg and then dredge in the caster sugar. Place on the baking sheet and make three diagonal cuts across each cake. Bake for 10-15 minutes or until golden brown. Let cool before eating.
You can store for 3 or 4 days at room temperature in a sealed container.

Old Elizabethan Recipe for Cambridge Almond Butter

Take a Quart of Cream and sixteen Eggs well beaten, mix them together and strain them into a Posnet, set them on a soft fire, and stir them continually; when it is ready to boil, put in half a quarter of a Pint of Sack, and stir it till it run to a Curd, then strain the Whey from it as much as may be, then beat four Ounces of blanched Almonds with Rosewater, then put the Curd and beaten Almonds and half a pound of fine Sugar into a Mortar, and beat them well together, then put it into Glasses and eat it with bread, it will keep a Fortnight

Updated:

Take a quart of cream, and half a pound of almonds, beat them with the cream, then strain it, and boil it with twelve yolks of eggs and two whites, till it curdle, hang it up in a cloth till morning and then sweeten it; you may rub it through a sieve with the back of a spoon, or strain it through a coarse cloth.

Images from pgs. 77-81 from Shutterstock & Wikipedia

THE HISTORICAL FICTION COMPANY HIGHLY RECOMMENDED AWARD

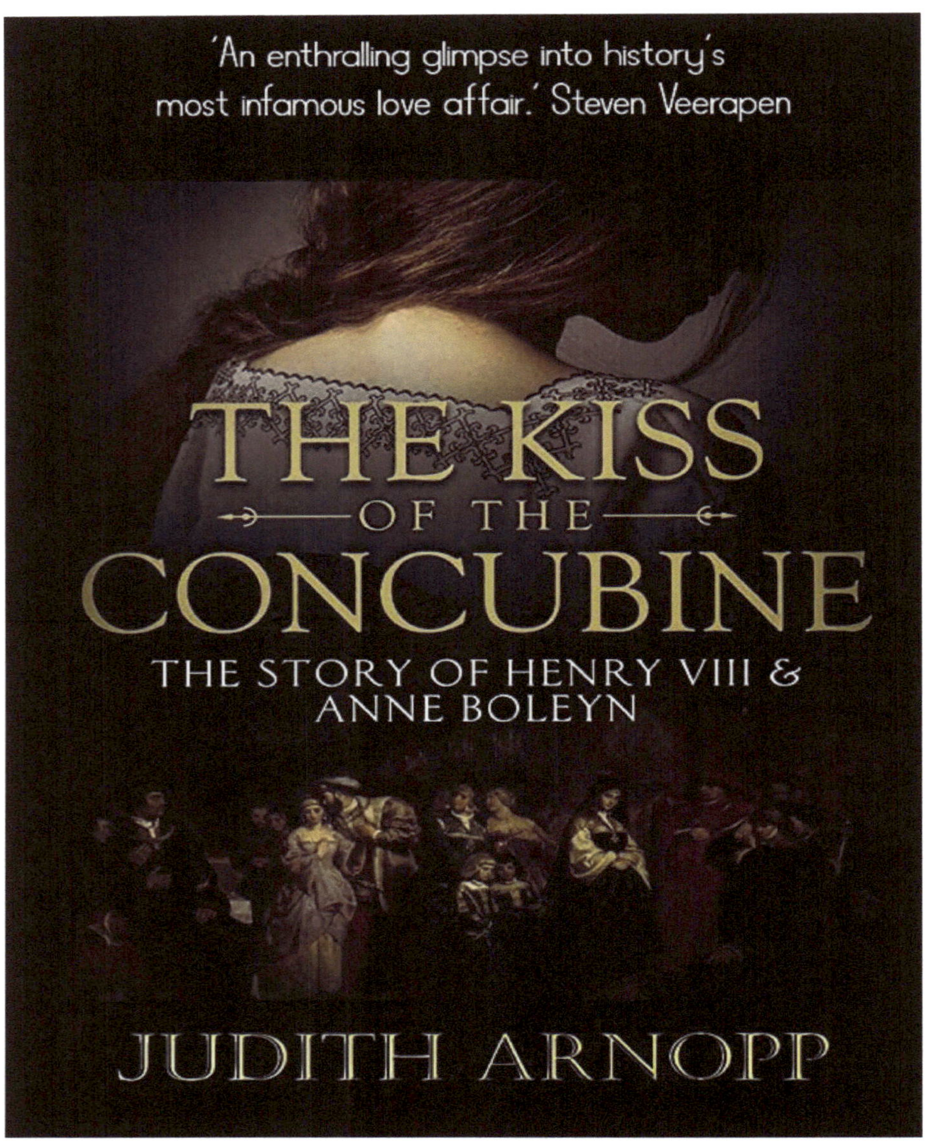

THE KISS OF THE CONCUBINE
Judith Arnopp

Winner of the 2022 Highly Recommended Award of Excellence and the Silver Category Winner for "Great Britain History"

There are moments when, as a reader, you know the second a book impacts you. And when that impact comes at the very beginning, well, you know you are about to take an exquisite journey. I have felt this many times throughout the years and when it happens, the books become dear to me, and a must-have for my own personal library. This is one of those times.

Reading the blurb, one might think this is just another re-telling of the infamous story of Anne Boleyn and Henry VIII, but I am here to say that this book transcends anything I have read to date on this popular subject. When you read lines such as: "...The king's eyes fly open and his eyeballs swivel from side to side, his disintegrating ego peering as if through the slits in a mummer's mask." or "Henry and I are the most powerful couple in all of England and yet, in the face of death, we are powerless," you are compelled to soak in every last detail. And last, I have to share this... "It is a dead sort of day, the type of day where the sky is white, and there is not even the hint of a breeze. Clouds muffle the horizon and I want to push them away, thrust back the oppression and the fear, and revel for one more day beneath blue skies, feel the wind on my cheeks, the scent of Hever in the air. Instead I am here, in my palatial prison, with no future, no next week to look forward to, perhaps not even a tomorrow."

Oh, there are so many many more for you to enjoy on this heavenly journey of words. This is just a small sampling.

The immense beauty of Judith Arnopp's selection of words and phrases is a lesson on how to write a historical novel. She takes what we already know of Anne and Henry to another level, a rare personal glimpse into their personalities, their fears, their hopes, and their love that turned England upside-down in terms of religion. In this book, Anne draws a reader's sympathy, as she is portrayed as a young naïve girl thrust down a path that ultimately brings her ruin. The delicate way the author shows Anne's love for her family home, Hever Castle, and the simplicities of that 'other life', the life before Henry, fleshes out her character and makes her tremendously relatable; as does the bond she shares with her brother, George, that is taken completely out of context by those wishing to destroy her.

The Kiss of the Concubine is now among my 'go-to' books that I will read again and again. Even this review does not do it justice. Simply put... get this book. It is stunning. A must-read!!

* * * * *

"By Jesu, Robert. You are an excellent spurrier and silversmith," said Richard. "I have not seen this quality of workmanship outside of London. You will make Rippon famous." He turned to Thomas, adding, "And you, my nephew, will wear spurs charged with Catholic spirit when we ride out. We cannot fail in our noble task now."

Talented spurrier Robert Gray has always admired his late father Alfred for taking part in the Pilgrimage of Grace many years ago, so he jumps at the chance to march alongside his own master in a rebellion against the heretic Queen Elizabeth in the autumn of 1569. As a staunch Catholic, taking part in this holy war would be a dream come true. He did not expect that dream would put his wife Catherine and their unborn child in mortal danger.

This novel is proof that there is never enough books about the Tudor era, and a plethora of hidden characters waiting to be revealed on the page. As the rebellion begins in Northeast England against Queen Elizabeth the First with the goal of re-establishing the Catholic faith and placing Mary, Queen of Scots, on the throne, a talented spurrier, Robert Grey, joins the cause. Both he and his wife, Catherine, are faithful Catholics, swearing loyalty to support the faith even at the risk of their own lives. Following in the footsteps of his own father who fought against Henry VIII's break from Rome, Robert's determination brings his wife, his unborn child, and himself close to danger as the threats mount.

The story unfolds, and betrayal surfaces when Robert's lifelong friend turns against him; and secrets of the past involving his father's death bubble to the surface causing great distress and many a sleepless night for Robert. Yet, even in this, he is determined to reveal all, even as the one person in opposition to him shows the same determination to keep them hidden.

In a fight for survival of their family, of friendships, and of honour, Robert and Catherine bind together to ensure their very lives... and all as the repercussions of Henry's rejection of the Catholic church come full force upon nobleman and commoner, alike.

Robert, like the majority of English Catholics of 1569, supported Mary's claim to the throne and viewed her as a way to restore the faith to England. In Northern England, several powerful nobles such as Charles Neville, 6th Earl of Westmorland, and Thomas Percy, 7th Earl of Northumberland, held fast to their Catholic faith and vowed an uprising against Queen Elizabeth. Robert joins in the rebellion, the same as his father before him had joined in the Pilgrimage of Grace against Henry VIII in 1536. Mary became their beacon of hope against the heretic.

There is so much vivid detail in this book that you are immediately drawn into the past, reliving a time when loyalty is tested and 'windows' are made into men's souls – Catholic against Protestant, and vice versa. With each decision made or side chosen, the shadows lurk ready to betray those who hold fast to their

Catholic leanings, those hiding their rosaries in secret places and holding mass with whispers.

Yet, Robert and Catherine's love and strength, supporting each other through this time as they stand united in their convictions, is a nod to the beauty and courage of unshakeable faith, even with the heat of betrayal breathing down their neck.

Without giving anything away, I must say that the world-building and the author's gift of story-telling is astounding and transports the reader to the stage of sixteenth century England and Scotland with very believable characters and natural dialogue befitting the time period. So meticulously researched and words chosen with finesse to create this story of their lives so as to immerse the reader in a world which, even though we know what happens from history, we find ourselves rooting for the main characters.

As relayed from the viewpoint of Robert and Catherine, the tragic events of October 1569 to January 1570 unfold. Robert, whose flair for metal work, especially his artistry for forging beautiful spurs in his village of Rippon; and his wife Catherine whose partial blindness does little to hinder her wide view of the events around them, even as she is labelled a witch, see their common life evolve as some of the key figures in the rebellion come into their life – Anne (also pregnant) and Thomas Percy (one of the leaders of the rebellion). Robert's master and patron, Thomas Markenfield, is first to join the conflict and Robert follows him, pledging loyalty and service to the Earls of Northumbria and Westmorland, while Catherine becomes a servant to Anne, Thomas's wife.

While history gives us the larger details of the rebellion, C. J. Richardson focuses the attention on the intimate way such conflicts change people's lives, and she does this in quite a skilful and sensitive way. What begins as excitement and the hopeful prospect of bringing back their former way of life develops from triumph to the ultimate failure of the uprising and the need for Robert to protect his family.

Some of my favourite vivid passages to give an overview of the author's artistry:

"The fog had lifted, and the winter sun tried to deceive us into thinking its rays cast warmth upon us, but its bright face served only to light up the ice on the rutted road and the newly formed icicles hanging from the boughs of the trees... She saw only the beauty of the landscape instead of feeling the bitter bite of the air around us. I knew it was because she was thinking about home in Rippon."

"There was a commotion outside. I could hear screaming and shouting. I got up and went to the window. The crowds were thick. Soldiers. Mary, Mother of God. The soldiers were rounding up men by the score and tying their hands together, using a rope to join them like a string of onions, then marching them to the obelisk on the market stede.... I looked down on the helmet of a soldier who had a taut rope fastened to his saddle, a limp body trailing through the dirty street behind him."

Vivid imagery worthy of the "Highly Recommended" award from The Historical Fiction Company and five stars!! Congratulations to the author for this fine work of art of the Tudor era.

* * * * *

ALL MANNER OF THINGS
by Wendy J. Dunn

Winter, 1539: María de Salinas is dying. Too ill to travel, she writes a letter to her daughter Katherine, the young duchess of Suffolk. A letter telling of her life: a life intertwined with her friend and cousin Catalina of Aragon, the youngest child of Isabel of Castile. It is a letter to help her daughter understand the choices she has made in her life, beginning from the time she keeps her vow to Catalina to share her life of exile in England. Friendship. Betrayal. Hatred. Forgiveness. Love wins out in the end.

The year is 1501 and a retinue of retainers and attendants is accompanying the royal daughter of Spain, Catalina of Aragon, from Spain to England where she will meet and wed the heir to the English throne, the young Prince Arthur Tudor, son of Henry VII. Among her attendants is her dearest friend María de Salinas, who brings with her a love of music and poetry and a rich knowledge of herbalism and healing. Maria and Catalina are all of fifteen years old at this point, just past childhood, but nonetheless pawns match of alliances and pacts between the great powers of sixteenth-century Europe.

All Manner of Things is the second book in the series Falling Pomegranate Seeds, which traces the life of Catalina of Aragon, youngest daughter of King Ferdinand of Aragon and Queen Isabella of Castile.

The story is told through María's eyes as, towards the end of her life, she pens a letter to her daughter. Through her recollections, her own letters to her tutor back in Spain, poetry, and a selection of texts from the period, we accompany her through the years. It is her own story that she tells to her daughter, but it is not only her story, for as one of Catalina's noble serving women, Maria's story is inextricably entwined with that of the princess.

Thus it is that the reader joins the royal retinue, moving from those first days of separation from family and everything they know, to England's cold and foreign shores, to life under the protection – or is that imprisonment? – of Henry Tudor. Maria stays with her dear friend during a short and heartbreaking half-marriage with gentle Prince Arthur, and through a tumultuous second marriage to the young and brash new king of England, Henry VIII, when she becomes known to her people as Queen Katherine, and to the history books as Katherine of Aragon.

Author Wendy J. Dunn paints an exquisitely detailed picture of the English court at the time. She brings us into the castles and courts of the kings where we meet stern and forbidding Henry Tudor and his compassionate wife. We celebrate the growing affection between Catalina and Arthur and grieve with the princess at her royal husband's death. And then, through years of spiteful neglect, we struggle with the Spanish contingent as they exist in a strained limbo, Catalina being neither wife nor widow, playthings to the men of power as they work their machinations of politics.

Likewise, we are witness to the casual brutality and violence of Henry VIII's regime once he takes power, and cry with the new queen with each lost baby as she watches her new husband's affection ebb in his quest for passion and an heir. And all around, the politics swirls, touching the edges of the narrative with its relentlessness, casting the powerlessness of the women into sharp relief.

This, Dr. Dunn accomplishes with a deft hand. Under the guidance of her pen, the men and women from our history books take on real life. Through meticulous research and skilled characterization, they become flesh and blood, cruel and kind, selfish and loving, and very real. She also takes the convoluted political manoeuvrings of the early sixteenth century and frames them in a context that renders them immediate and comprehensible. All those alliances and pacts and agreements that cover the pages of our textbooks are made real on the pages of her book. These actors are not an assortment of names and titles, but they are Catalina's kin. And as Catalina discovers her place in this world of shifting alliances, so too does María come to terms with her own fate, and that of her family.

While the narrative arc of *All Manner of Things* is as carefully constructed as any novel, the main events are true and the characters were real people. Catalina, of course, was Henry VIII's first wife, and María was indeed one of her attendants. And as Catalina grows from timid and superstitious girl into a woman fit to be Queen of England, so does María grow. Her final act of love towards her friend – no spoilers – shows how strong her difficult life made her. This, too, was a real event. María, it seems, might have been a pawn in the hands of the powerful men around her, but she was not one to just give up, and we love her more for it.

My quibbles about this book are few and far between. It was, perhaps, a bit slow at the beginning, and I would have liked to know more about María's life after her marriage, although that was not the focus of the story. There were also one or two small threads of narrative that were left unresolved, tensions raised and then abandoned. But these were very minor issues, more of a wish-list than a litany of complaints.

In sum, I can think of almost nothing I would change about this book. It is beautifully written with realistic and sympathetic characters, and shot through with the golden threads of music and poetry that bring the era to full life. If Tudor history is your passion – or even if it's not – this is a book to enjoy again and again.

Five Stars from The Historical Fiction Company, "Highly Recommended" Award

*　*　*　*　*

SONGBIRD
by Karen Heenan

What a way to retell a story about King Henry VIII and Anne Boleyn!! If you've ever wanted to know about the inner workings of the household, told from a servant's POV, one who was closely linked to the infamous King and his wives, well, this is the book to get. This is the story of Bess Davydd, a young girl bought by Henry VIII to become a minstrel for his court, a songstress whose voice is as a nightingales. During the storyline, you are offered brief glimpses and encounters with the royals (i.e. Henry and Anne) but the story is much more about Bess and her love interests – Tom, another bought minstrel, and Nick, a nobleman. The story is compact, well-developed, and stretches into the depths of emotions separating commoners from the high-born, as well as showing the commonality, the human element. If I have one negative, and perhaps it is only from my POV, I struggled with wrapping my head around her age, of how young she is when she starts to experience "love" and with her sounding like a woman at the age of ten to fourteen. I mean, I get it, I know from my own research into history that girls at that age and in that time period were wives and mothers by the time they were

fourteen, even younger, but I did struggle a bit with it. However, my own feelings did not overwhelm the overall story, to which I enjoyed thoroughly. I give this book five stars and will highly recommend to anyone who loves books about the Tudor era.

* * * * *

THE CONJURER'S APPRENTICE
by G. J. Williams

One day, the body of a stable boy serving Lord Cecil's household shows up on the banks of the river Thames in London with a yellow woolen ribbon on his body. John Dee, a mathematician and astronomer is called to investigate the corpse and explore the circumstances. By his side is Margaretta Morgan, a young apprentice disguised as a maid.

It is 1555 London, and the rumor is that Mary Tudor, the queen of England, is pregnant and expected to give birth soon. Her sister Elizabeth has been summoned to assist and witness the birth, thus giving up any hopes that one day she may claim the throne for her-

self. Queen Mary, who had restored Catholicism in the English kingdom, had married prince Philip of Spain, whom she loved very much.

These are the settings of G. J. Williams's murder mystery novel, The Conjuror's Apprentice, where the detective is a sorcerer and his apprentice an empath, abilities both dangerous and thrilling.

From the first pages, I knew the book was different from other crime books I read, not only because it takes place in 16thcentury England, a time of turbulence and struggles for power, but because Margaretta, the protagonist, has a rare talent. This she needs to cultivate on the street of London, witnessing the persecution and execution of believers of the Protestant faith that opposed the Catholics. When he sends her out, her teacher John Dee thinks this is the best way to learn.

"If you are to hone your gift, you have to understand the full spectrum of men's feelings, fears, and fallacious thoughts. The good, the evil, the kind, the cruel, the intelligent and the witless. It is all part of our soul and you need to see them all."

Thus, she can help John Dee solve the mystery and expose the criminal. But the crimes continue as the two uncover clues incriminating royal family members and overseas spy agents. Their investigation relies only on interviewing witnesses and collecting evidence. None of the modern forensic techniques were available to them. But what they have proved to be more valuable: a handful of crystals and a deck of tarot cards, mastered by John Dee, and the gift of mind reading that Margaretta possesses. They use these tools only sparsely as they can also kill.

With a keen eye for historical accuracy, the author portrays her characters with a fine brush, giving them distinct personalities and strong voices. Our protagonist,

Margaretta, is only nineteen years old, but she's witty and humble at the same time. And when the stakes are high, by the end of the book, her courage saves not only the day but the future of the English royalty. But Margaretta is not an ordinary girl, and she knows it.

"The doctor did my cards the day he found me and they told him I am an old soul. In the religion of our ancestors, they would believe I have been born many times and had walked this earth before in numerous guises. But we dare not to speak of such things these days for fear of being called heretic, conjuror, witch...all the names which strike fear into the soul in Queen Mary's terrible reign."

And indeed, these esoteric methods help Doctor Dee and Margaretta investigate and solve the series of crimes, and the two of them struggle to keep it a secret as their lives and loved ones' lives depend on it. But such gifts must come out and shine sooner or later, and that is when the plot diverges, higher stakes being now at play. However, the author skillfully ties up loose ends and stirs the readers to an ending that, although predictable to a history buff, has a satisfying ending and promises that the characters may return in another book in the series.

The novel is written in an alert and assertive tone, with episodes of inner dialog, and it is clear of unnecessary descriptions or filler dialog that sometimes clutter a book. To portray the people in their historical context, the author often uses historical details rather than archaic words, sometimes with an amusing result like this:

"Just as before, Lottie refused to wash as it was a church day. Not even Margaretta's insistence that she should try to smell sweet for Sam would shake her fear of water on Sundays."

G. J. Williams mastered the arching plot and character development by layering the subplots and intertwining the secondary characters, improving the storyline and making the experience more gratifying. And because the book is a well-crafted mystery with elements of romance, set in a thoroughly researched historical period, with some real characters, I would recommend the book to any reader of historical fiction.

The Conjurer's Apprentice by G. J. Williams receives five stars and the "Highly Recommended" award of excellence from The Historical Fiction Company

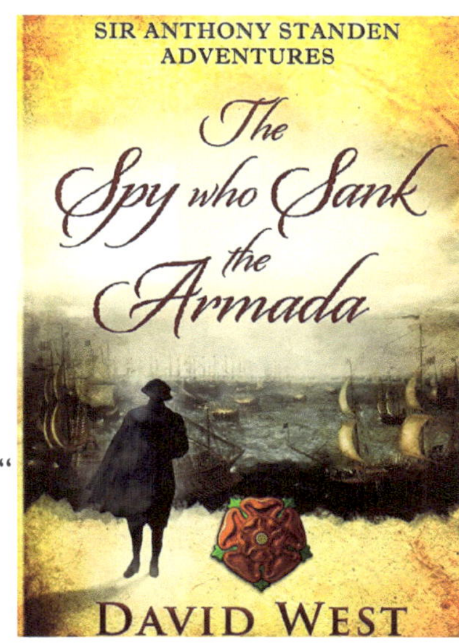

THE SPY WHO SANK THE ARMADA
by David West

'The Spy Who Sank the Armada' by David West is the first of three books devoted to the highly perilous life and times of Sir Anthony Standen, Tudor mercenary spy for hire; a man well in tune with the extremely fraught times in which he lived. This is a Tudor spy thriller, unabashed, unapologetic, and written in grand, pacey style!

The book is sweeping and certainly covers a great deal of territory in terms of geography and events and notable historical incidents. It is based on the actual and often mysterious life of an actual figure; Sir Anthony Standen [born c.1548 - ?] In his evidently crowded career, Standen, English born but a firm favourite within the circle of Mary, Queen of Scots [who appointed him a 'Master of Horse' and knighted him] flitted and flirted throughout Europe in the pay of a variety of very different spymasters. His travels took him from England and Scotland to France, to the contentious Lowlands, and to Italy and Spain and beyond. West's creation is a resourceful and indefatigable man; a sixteenth-century adventurer, a veritable 'James Bond' of his time.

We first meet the young Sir Anthony Standen in Paris in 1567 and seemingly at a bit of a loose end. His early attempts at espionage on behalf of the English end in failure and near death. Paris is a powder keg, with near and actual civil war between the French Catholic and Protestant Huguenot factions; and always the abiding English fear of Spanish involvement in their affairs - not only in England but also in Scotland..

The late sixteenth century is of course a crucial and fascinating period in European history. It is also very complicated, so we must thank David West for guiding the readers through the minefields of this period with considerable savoir-faire and dexterity, revealing a deep knowledge of and feel for his subject matter. At the English Embassy, he is turned over to various masters and adepts at the various black arts of espionage and young Anthony emerges as an accomplished creator and decipherer of codes and ciphers, an expert lockpicker and silent burglar, and a proficient killer; skills to add to a repertoire that already includes an extraordinary ability as a linguist and a flair for swordplay. Anthony is next commissioned by the up-and-coming Francis Walsingham, the new English Ambassador in Paris to spy on the Spanish and to gather information on their plans and intentions and this involved a very long period of activity in fighting for William of Orange, leader of the rebel Protestant forces in the Low Countries, specifically the famous maritime rebel force of 'the Sea Beggars'.

There is rarely a dull moment in the hectic life and career of Sir Anthony Standen and the reader's attention is always fixed upon him as he continues to be both an eyewitness and active participant in the major dramas of the period. Where events arrive at boiling point Standen can usually be relied upon to be centre stage or, at the very least, lurking in the shadows. The reader can only marvel at [and, perhaps, envy] the sheer, steady, cold nerve of the man or his uncanny ability to not only make the most of his circumstances but turn them to his best advantage, The resourceful Sir Anthony is a superlative survivor, dealt many bad hands and with more than seems fair and equitable of "chutzpah'. After leaving the 'Sea Beggars' and making the acquaintance of William of Orange [who also pays him] he burgles the house of an absent Governor and steals money and important documents, the contents of which he relays in code to his master Francis Walsingham. Surviving and escaping a full-blown Spanish attack and massacre of the inhabitants of a major town, he then masquerades as an Italian soldier in the Spanish army and becomes, naturally enough, a despatch rider entrusted with sensitive military information which he dutifully relays back to the English authorities in Paris. He in fact maintains this pretence for several years before being robbed and left unconscious. Naturally enough, he is recognised and taken in by a beautiful widow to whom he had once done a favour in a previous life when he had been Antonio Foscari, an Italian wine merchant - his previous cover back in his Paris days. They become lovers and it is a fine enough life until one morning when her illegitimate son whom she has been separated from for many years comes to call. This man turns out to be none other than the new

Spanish Governor. Anticipating Henry Fielding's 'Tom Jones' by a good century and a half, he makes a hasty exit in a state of some undress through the window and makes off on the Governor's prized stallion, thus making him the most wanted man in the Lowlands. He sets off, hotly pursued, across the length and breadth of Spanish-controlled Europe, heading for the safety of the land of the Ottomans and the fabulous City of Constantinople. As previously noted, 'never a dull moment'. This book [and in all likelihood, the following ones in the series] would equally make an excellent action comic book or television serial! The reader needs to bear in mind at all times that all these adventures are based on the life of a real person! Sir Anthony Standen inhabits his world like some inverted, world-weary, and cynical 'Candide'. In the words of Shakespeare "bestriding the narrow world like a Colossus."

At the risk of falling into the trap of simply narrating, a very pleasant interlude of four years follows as a guest of the Sultan in the Topkapi Palace where Anthony adds written and spoken Arabic to his already impressive portfolio of accomplishments and develops an appreciation of both alchemy and medicine [and poisons!] through his study of Arabic texts. At one point he pauses to reflect upon the possibilities of developing a business in the cultivation of tulip bulbs, foreshadowing a phenomenon in the Lowlands in the following century. He also sends frequent and highly informative letters to Walsingham ever anxious to stir up trouble for the Spanish. Ever since the catastrophic defeat of the Turks at the sea battle of Lepanto by the Spanish and Venetians the Turks are not inclined to take an affectionate view of the Spanish. In his last communication, Walsingham orders Anthony to Florence and the Court of Duke Francis de Medici where it is hoped that a shared connection with Mary Queen of Scots can be exploited, for there is evidence of a plot to murder Queen Elizabeth. And it is here at

the glittering Florentine Court and by deploying all of his considerable skills that Sir Anthony Standen uncovers a plot in his greatest triumph to date. This, in his subsequent stay there and in Madrid, is just one of his many activities.

Those thinking that perhaps too much of the plot has already been revealed may rest assured. That which has been already outlined is but a fraction of what is still yet to come in the chaotic career of Sir Anthony Standen. Everything thus far is something of a trifle in comparison with what is yet to occur in the political hotspots of Florence, Madrid, London, and Rome!

There are confrontations with Kings and Popes and extraordinary figures such as Cecil and the Earl of Essex and a knighthood from Queen Elizabeth still to come. In separate conversations with both the new King James I, the life of whose mother Standen had saved so many years before, and Pope Clement VIII both these eminent figures remark on what an interesting life Holden appears to have led. This is, of course, something of an understatement, given the circumstances. Sir Anthony Standen has to be just about the most travelled man of his age. He has been both the welcome bidden guest and the hidden and illicit lurker and intruder in most of the grand Palaces and Courts of Europe; as well as the unwilling inmate of most of its more infamous gaols, up to and including the Tower of London. He has been both the paid and unpaid agent and double agent of all the competing powers and has won and lost small fortunes several times over. He has been betrayed and double-crossed by most of them as well, but survives on each occasion to spy again.

In 1605, at the end of this admirable first book, we find him living on Papal patrimony in a beautiful villa with lands with his wife [whom he had met years before in Florence and whose subsequent Wedding was conducted by the Pope] and his three children. West does not tell us if he has white hair and shaking limbs, but he certainly deserves to have these bequests of his life to date. If he now hopes to spend his declining years tending his vines in the bosom of his doting family he is to be sorely disappointed when an Italian Cardinal, an old associate, arrives dangling a purse of 2000 ducats and a new mission. We are not told the nature of the task, but it is patently clear that he must put his plans on hold for a while and once more brush up on his old highly advanced skills of forgery, lock picking, and swordplay and don afresh his chameleon-like Actor's mask.

This is a fine and stirring tale indeed and bodes well for the following books charting the further life and times of Sir Anthony Standen. From the relatively few known verifiable facts regarding the life of the man, David West has conjured up an epic portrayal of a truly 'Renaissance' figure [at one point he reveals a skill of draughtsmanship and portraiture]; a nerveless and cold-blooded 'Maestro' of his chosen profession. The book is peppered with the emergence and frequent re-emergence of notable historical figures who, again in the style of 'Candide', display a habit of appearing with unfortunate results. In telling this story the author has clearly been scrupulous in his attention to the welter of confusing and often seemingly contradictory information that surrounds this complex and fascinating period of European history that may have the beneficial effect of persuading readers to carry out their own research. 'The spy who sank the Armada' is a fine read and accomplishment and bodes well for its s u c c e s s o r s .

*   *   *   *   *

"The Spy Who Sank the Armada" receives 4.5 stars from The Historical Fiction Company

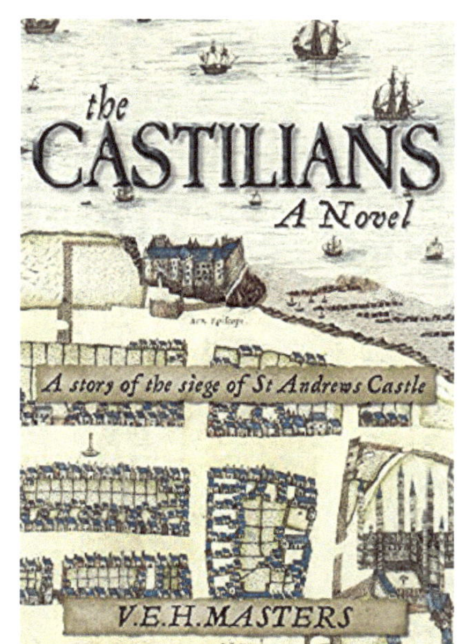

THE CASTILIANS
by V.E.H. Masters

The year is 1546 and Scotland is under attack from Henry VIII, determined to marry his son, Edward, to the infant Mary, Queen of Scots. A few among the Scottish nobles, for both political and religious reasons, are eager for this alliance, as well. The story begins with a brutal killing, a necessary one in the eyes of those seeking this union, as they kill Cardinal Beaton, Mary's great protector, in retaliation for the burning of George Wishart, an advocate for the new Protestant faith, and they capture St Andrews Castle, with hopes of a rescue from the King of England. While you expect this story to cleave to the historical details, which it does with great finesse, this actually becomes a story about a brother and sister, two young people trying to find their way in the midst of the political and religious upheaval surrounding them. Will is one of the Castilians, fighting for the Protestant cause, even as he is disturbed at the horrific handling of Beaton's murder and questions the tactics on more than one occasion. But he is loyal, and this is his strong suit during the entire story, even though his actions bring a shadow over his family, a family still caught in the middle of faithfulness to Rome and listening to the powerful words of zealots like John Knox. Bethia, his sister, suffers from her brother's actions in that her father thinks to marry her off quickly before anyone discovers that his son, Will, is party to the uprising. He is a man willing to use his daughter as a financial pawn, attaching her to a man who might give the family a bit of clout, and ignoring any thought of his daughter's wishes; such was the way in the time period when women were viewed as mere chattel. Loyalty is a huge theme in this novel – how hard will you fight for something you believe in? So often Will is given the chance to escape, often times urged by his Bethia, but his religious convictions remain powerful, even as his strength withers away in the midst of sickness, disease, and starvation. Bethia's loyalty to her brother, in trying to protect him, brings her to the brink of her own struggle for survival. Ultimately, both of them must make choices that set them on their future course... which also sets the stage for more novels to follow in their journey (I hope!) The historical events of the siege of St Andrews Castle, and the murder of Cardinal Beaton, is a story I did not know much about since so many historical novels lean more towards the spectacular court of Henry Tudor and his six wives – and I applaud Ms Masters for taking on this story. I also loved that she used the point of view of these two young people, adding details about a typical Scottish family during the time period, day-to-day concerns and pursuits, and their own worries when it came to politics and religion. Teenagers in Tudor Scotland transforming into strong adults with sturdy opinions about their own future and the future of Scotland - what a great setting! The use of Scottish words and phrasing added a great flair to the book, perfect authenticity, and made the characters come alive from the page – I enjoyed this aspect very much. My only critical analysis is the use of the present tense voice. I must admit that I am not a huge fan of this type of writing. Sometimes I was quite thrown-off by this, especially in the beginning when I felt myself having to push through the story in order to get to the thick of things. After settling into this narrative, I started to enjoy the story and more so upon reaching Bethia's struggle to escape the castle. This descriptive passage was enthralling and gripping, well worth the effort of pushing through the choice of tense choice. Another aspect I enjoyed was the comparison of the two religious men in the novel – John Knox and Cardinal Beaton. You see two religious devotees from the perspective of these two teenagers, of a man steeped in hypocrisy with his mistress and bastards, carried from place to place with his brash four-poster bed, and red Papal robes, against the red-faced, spittle-spraying trumpeting wordy speeches of a zealot; neither of which you might think engender endearment to their side of the church aisle, yet they do – somehow. We are given a commoner's glimpse into the splitting of God and worship in 16th-century Scotland, along with the gruesome details of what each side was willing to do to push forward their ideas – stake-burning and fear on one side, and revolution/reformation/murder on the other. All of this is developed very successfully and flanked by the search for love in the midst of all this chaos. Bethia and her friend, Elspeth, eye each young man as a future prospective husband, just as any young teenage girls would do, giggling over the pros and cons of each; and the soft storyline of Bethia and her first crush brings a sweetness to the harsh realities around them. But, as with most teenage romances, both girls suffer heartbreak and the consequences of their actions, as well as the choices of their families. The outcome after the siege of St Andrews for both Will and Bethia is surprising and one I dare not give away. Readers looking for a different story about Tudor history will enjoy this well-written tale!

**PURSUING A
MASTERPIECE
by Sandra Vasoli**

In Pursuing a Masterpiece by Sandra Vasoli, Zara Rossi is an American Ph.D. student studying in Rome. Her Ph.D. studies are focused on Henry VIII's break with the Roman Catholic Church. During a visit to the Papal Archives, Rossi uncovers an old letter warning Pope Clement VII about a portrait of Henry VIII and Anne Boleyn that contains clues to a conspiracy that could be catastrophic and history-altering if Rossi is correct. Rossi's research is combined into a dual storyline where readers are transported back to the Tudor time period where they will meet characters such as Henry VIII and Thomas Cromwell. Hans Holbein and his art are considered as well as many other political elements of the time period. It becomes nearly impossible to pull yourself away from either timeline as you root for Rossi and her research and become enthralled in the conception of the infamous painting. It is a complex novel and story that is so well done and is enjoyable to read.

"Volumes filled with Coptic Greek, illuminated medieval manuscripts still vivid with color deposited by monks many hundreds of years ago, and at the front of the room, three women unrolling parchments on which were drawn the original architectural plans for the façade of St. Peter's Basilica."

Pursuing a Masterpiece has two different timelines. One is set in the present as Zara is conducting her research and trying to identify the meaning of the information that she is finding. The second timeline is that of the Tudor Era mostly in Henry VIII's court surrounding the situation in which Anne Boleyn and Henry VIII are pursuing a relationship that results in England's separation from teh Catholic Church. That timeline progresses from there and the reader is able to follow the painting's journey through history. Each timeline is equally compelling and exciting to read. Vasoli writes both of these timelines so well because of the research that she has clearly put in. The historical timeline as well as the art and historical references throughout the book are accurate, well-researched, and well-explained in a nuanced way that the reader will barely even realize that they may in fact be learning history as they read. Readers will appreciate the evident love for history that Vasoli has as well as her excellent research that is so evident throughout the book.

"Alone in Whitehall's magnificent library, Hans paced; his footfalls echoing on the polished floor; mouth so dry that no amount of ale could quench it. At moments he felt as if he might vomit, so he sat to pour himself a sizable beaker of wine and swallowed it in two gulps, hoping it would settle his lurching stomach and bolster his courage."

Taking on such looming historical characters as Henry VIII and Anne Boleyn can be a daunting task for any author. This requires an author to create a version of these historical entities that are both believable and relatable for readers while honoring history. Vasoli does this beautifully. She clearly understands these characters and what life would have most likely been like for them. She also creates a more modern character in Zara Rossi but she is no less awe-inspiring than the famous counterparts she shares the pages with. Rossi is relatable and the perfect protagonist.

The manuscript is incredibly clean and well edited and the writing is pleasurable to read. The writing style is mature and well-developed making it easy to read and follow. While the prose is nothing over the top in style, the author has used it appropriately to develop a story that will appeal to a wide variety of readers. Vasoli is skilled at using foreshadowing appropriately and keeping the mystery alive and engrossing throughout her novel. However, the real gem of Vasoli's writing is her ability to weave imagery throughout the novel so that the art pieces, settings, and characters come alive with rich detail. The reader should not find themselves losing interest in the story or the writing style. Readers will also find that the pacing of the story is excellent. The mystery elements of the story are effective at keeping readers interested and constantly wanting to find out more.

"In May of 1536, ugly accusations about the Queen's rumored infidelity had swirled about court. The maniacal King turned his back on a wife he'd once adored, condemning her, along with her five falsely accused lovers, to death by beheading. The otherwise delightful English month of May became gruesome with blood spilled by those whom the King had once cherished. "

Pursuing a Masterpiece is the perfect book for readers who love historical fiction and mysteries with a touch of thriller elements. It blends these genres together perfectly in a way that creates a story that is nearly impossible to put down. Those with an affection for art will also enjoy this book. The author does a fantastic job of explaining the history and implications in detail so even those not familiar with much of the historical references will be able to understand and follow the story. The book is rather lengthy at just about 600 pages. Casual readers may struggle with a book this size but it is well worth the effort and time to read. Some readers may also struggle with the dual timelines that are present in Pursuing a Masterpiece.

"Antonio and I arrived at Hever on a chilly and drizzly afternoon. The mist, although shrouding early blooms in the gardens, enhanced the dreamlike aura which clings undeniably to the exquisite Castle, moat, and surroundings."

Fans of the Tudor time period, art, and mysteries, in particular, will love this book and enjoy getting lost in the story. Vasoli is a master at creating dual timelines that are both engrossing and complement each other beautifully. A dual timeline that will pull readers in, a thrilling mystery, and excellent, extensive research make Pursuing a Masterpiece an engrossing story that readers won't be able to put down.

*   *   *   *   *

"Pursuing a Masterpiece" by Sandra Vasoli receives 4.5 stars from The Historical Fiction Company

ENTER TO WIN $1000 AT THE HFC BOOK OF THE YEAR AWARDS!

Go to thehistoricalfictioncompany.com/ award-submissions

"

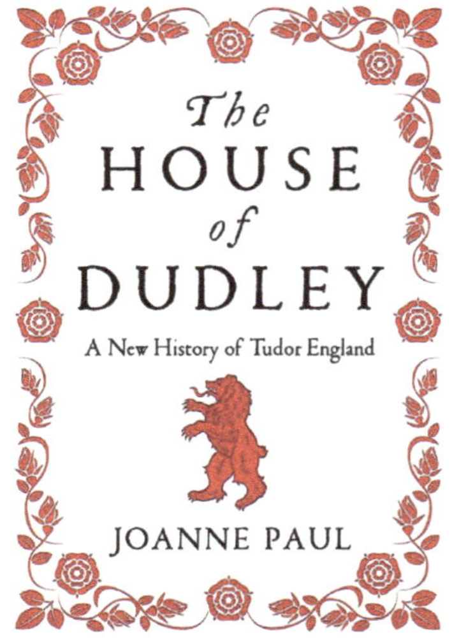

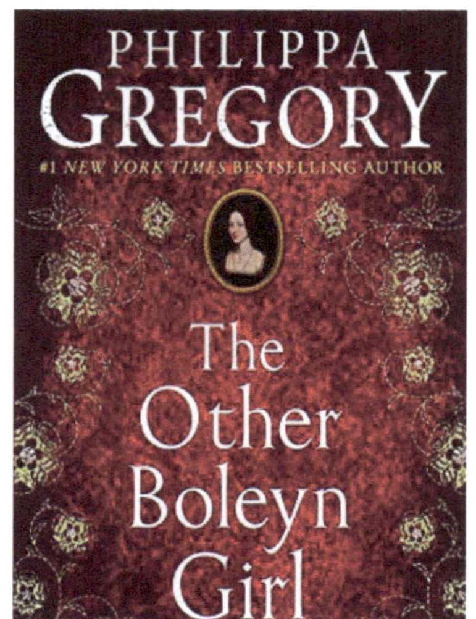

AVAILABLE FOR
PURCHASE
AT AMAZON or
the HFC
BOOKSHOP.

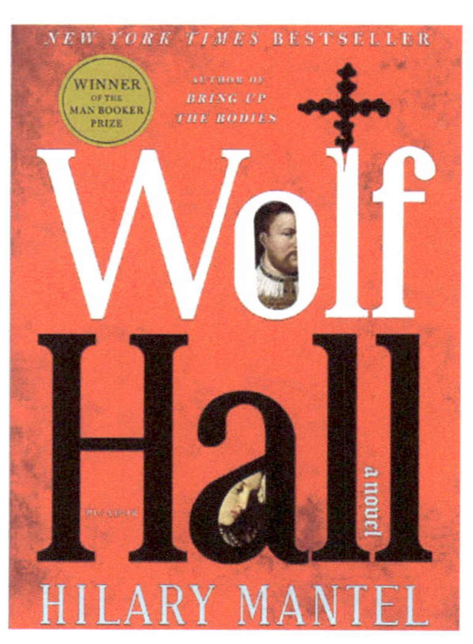

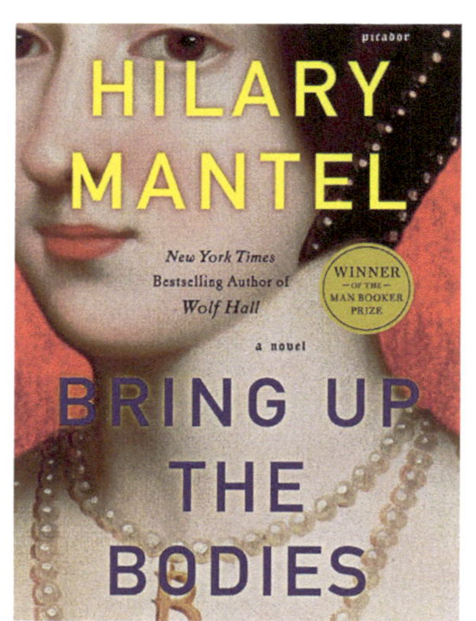

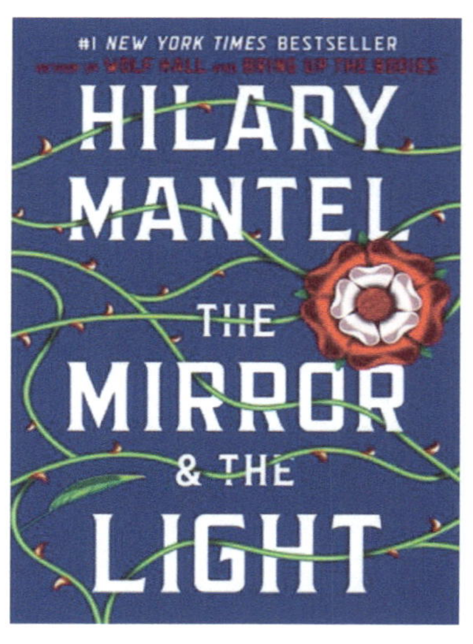

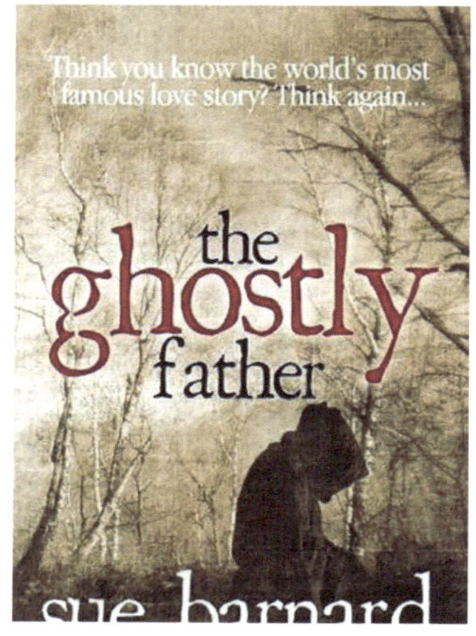

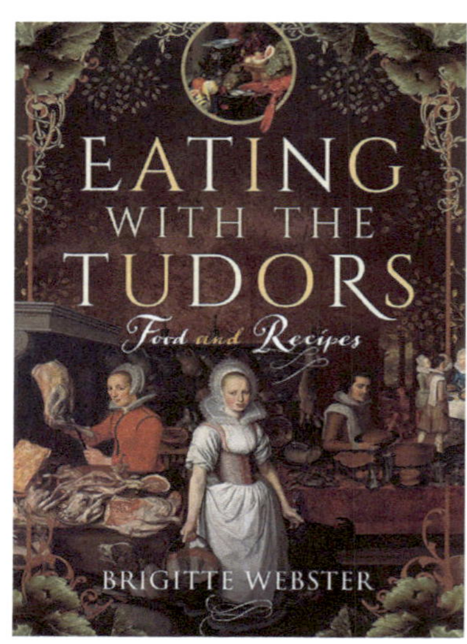

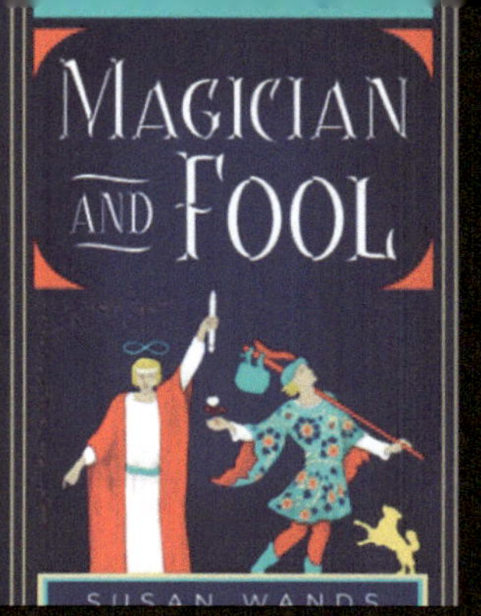

Considered an oddball in Victorian society, Pamela will have to learn to conjure her own magic to protect her muses.

BUY TODAY AT AMAZON

1910: Italian immigrants are pouring into New England by the thousands every year. They bring with them their own culture and their own form of justice from the Old World. Tenuous finances, unscrupulous con-men and a desperate need to achieve the American Dream all work together to put Giuseppe Amato into a desperate position! How far will Joe and his family go to get their share of the dream?

BUY TODAY AT AMAZON

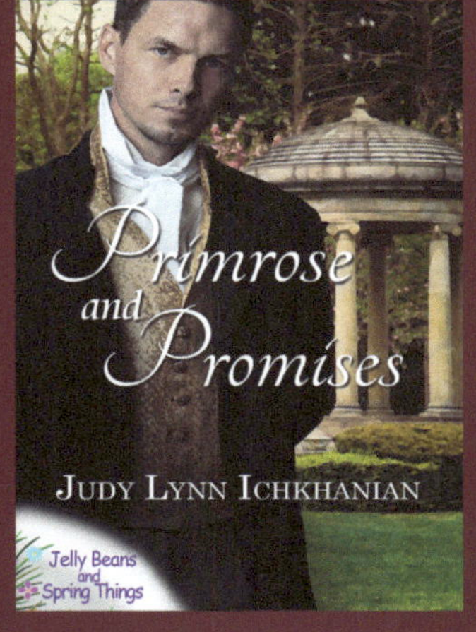

Wooed with jellied plops and farce, how could any Victorian heroine resist the Viscount's charms?

Buy today at AMZN

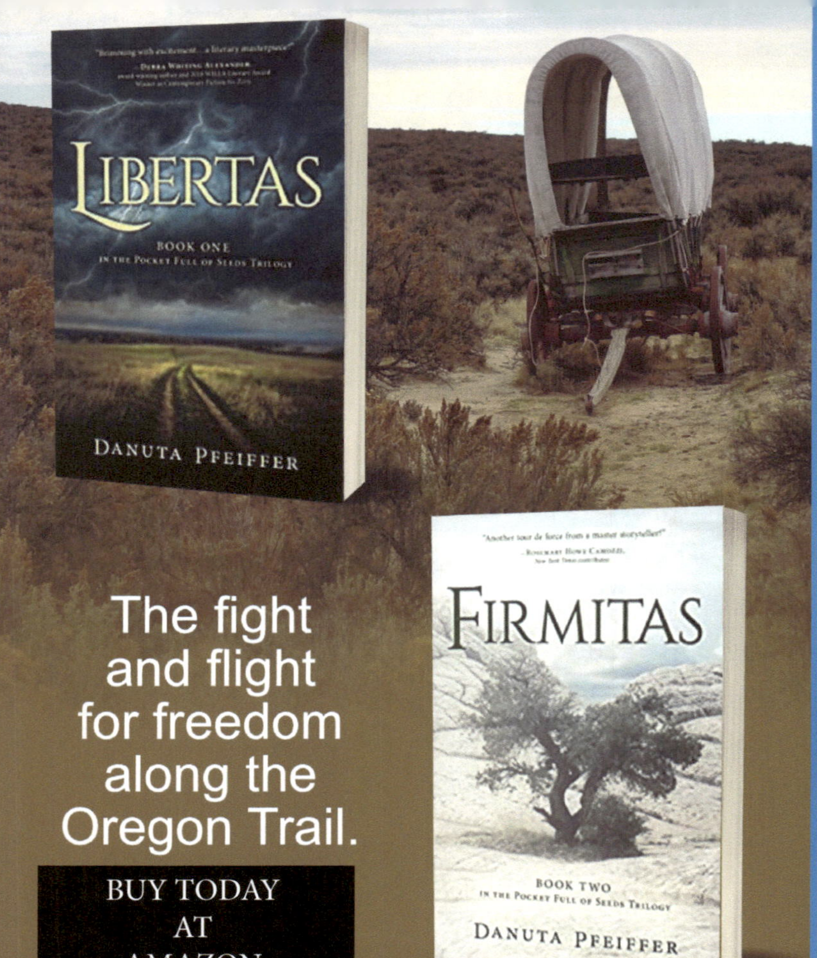

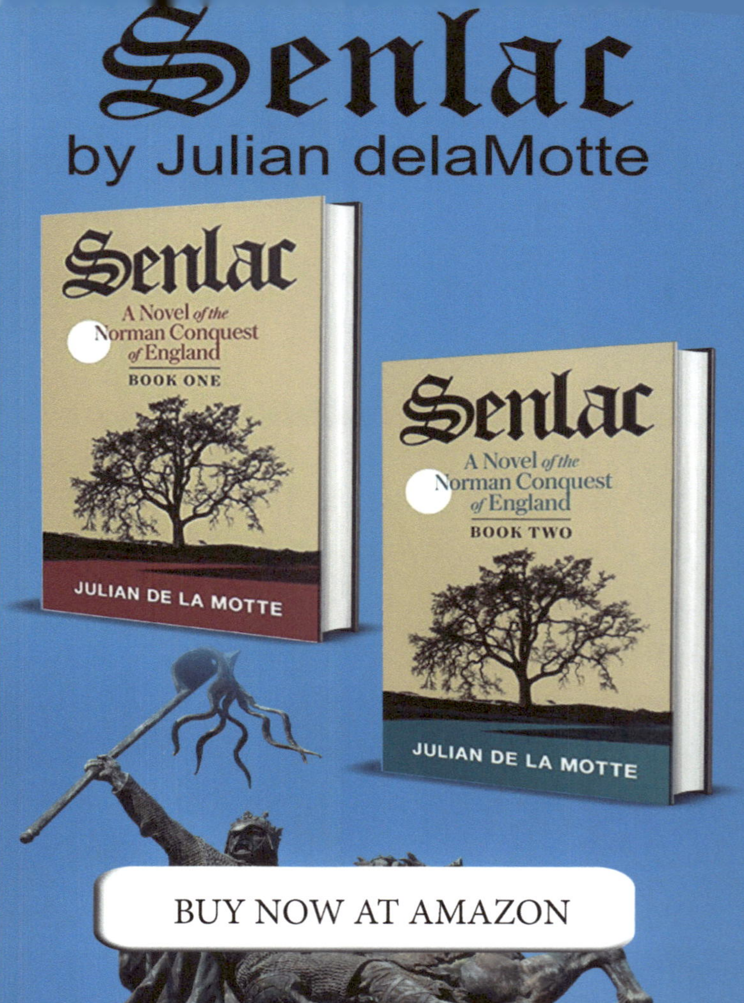

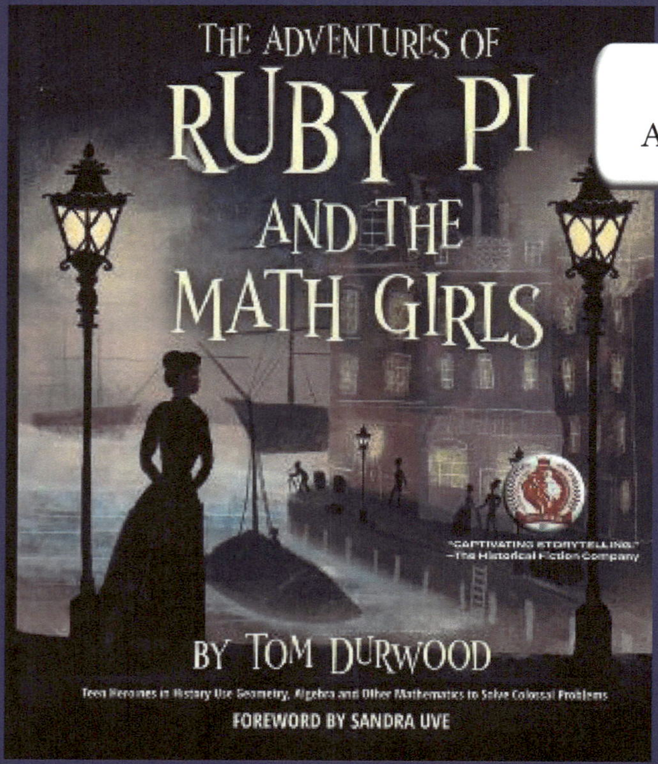

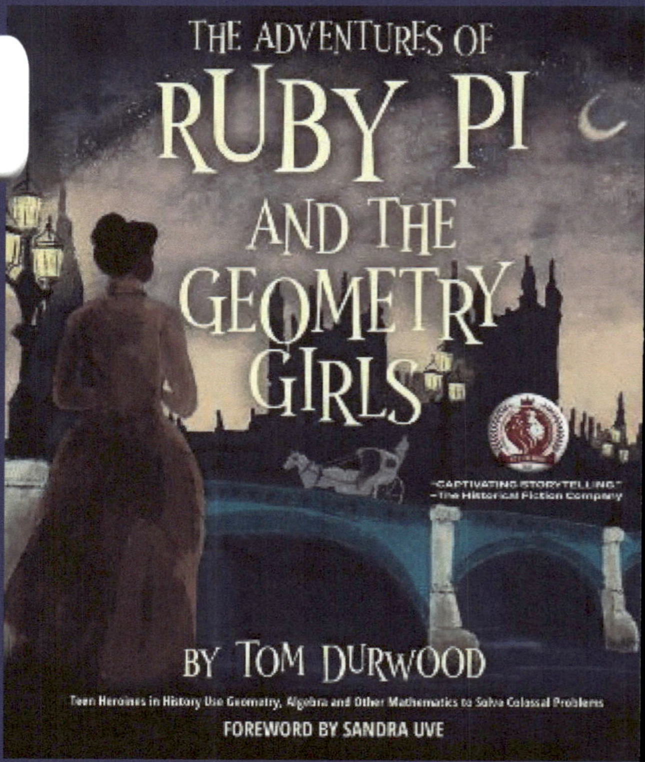

Teen Heroines in History Use Geometry, Algebra, and Other Mathematics to Solve Colossal Problems